Copyright © 2013 C.
Cover design by: Davida Baldwin
Editor: Twenty First Street Urban Editing

All rights reserved. Without limiting the rights under copyright reserved above. No part of this book may be reproduced, stored in, or introduced into a retrieval system or transmitted in any form, or by any means (electronic, mechanical, photocopying, recording, or otherwise), without prior written consent from the author except brief quotes used in reviews.

This is a work of fiction. It is not meant to depict, portray, or represent any real persons. Names, characters, places, or incidents are either the product of the author's imagination or are used fictitiously, and any resemblance to actual persons living or dead, business establishments, events, or locales is entirely coincidental.

Next Door Nympho 2

C.J Hudson

Next Door Nympho 2

Next Door Nympho 2

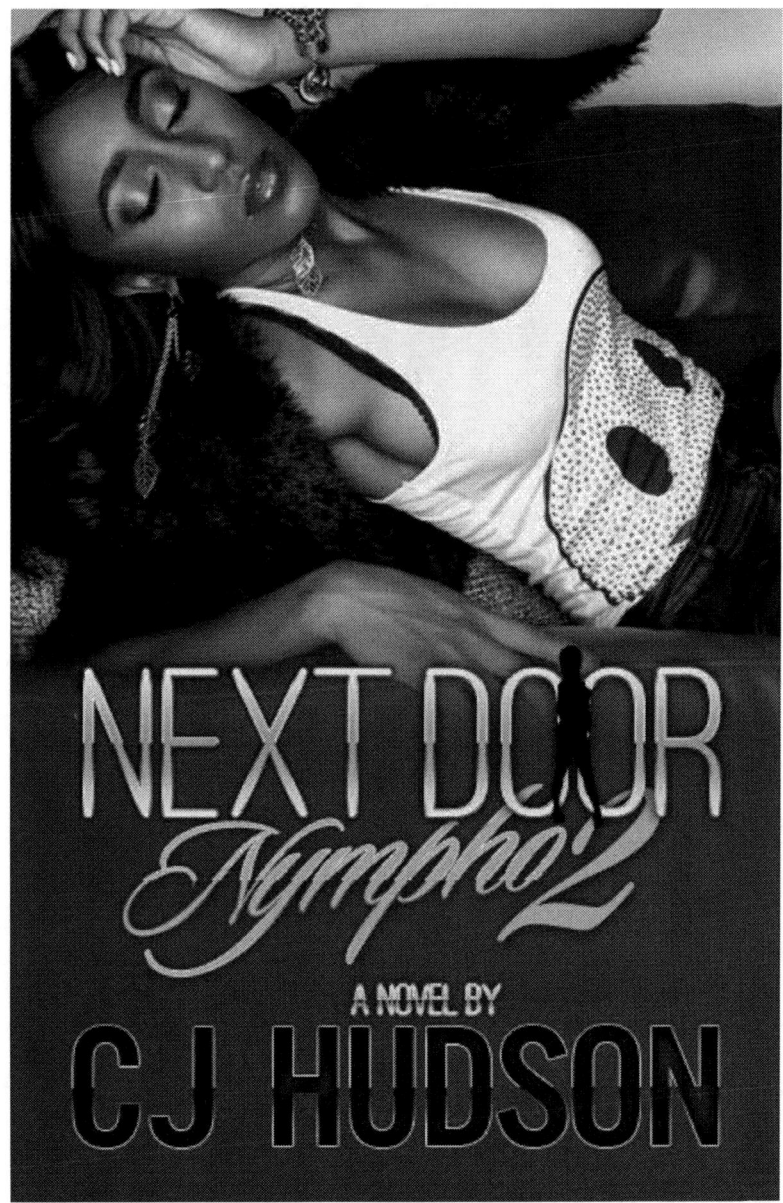

Next Door Nympho 2

1
Candice

I got his ass now, I thought to myself. Don't get me wrong though. Professor Reynolds had been quite the challenge. It had taken me some time to wear his fine ass down. It was a good thing to, because after flunking another test combined with my failure to turn in the last three homework assignments, I was flunking my sociology class something terrible.

But thanks to special talents, that I was sure that I'd inherited from my mother, my grade would soon be changed for the better. Slyly I cut my eyes towards the door. I left it unlocked on purpose, just in case the good professor tried to renege on our agreement. My roommate, Toi had been there the entire time and was taping the encounter.

At first, she'd doubted my skills.

'Bitch please', she'd said. *'That man is a professional. You'll never catch him slippin' like that.'*

But like I told her ass, there not a muthafucka alive who could resist Sprung, the moniker that I'd given to my pussy. The name is self-explanatory. Toi, after noticing that I was checking to see if she was still there, gave me the thumbs up. I smiled slightly, knowing that everything was being taken care of. It was funny to me sometimes how this bitch would try to give me advice.

When Toi first got here, she didn't know a dick from a dildo. Her sheltered ass was blind to the fuck game, until yours truly opened her eyes. The bitch can now suck two dicks at one time. But my roommate and now best friend still had a lot to learn about sex. Maybe after watching my performance she would pick up a few things and realize that Candice Robinson ain't no joke. Professor Reynolds grabbed the back of my head roughly.

With both hands, he tried to force all eight inches of his man meat down my throat. It was obvious that this nigga was trying to make me gag but he had me fucked up. I was a thoroughbred. My gag reflex was virtually non-existent, and although he was holding a pretty decent sized package, it was gonna take more inches than he had to make me cry Uncle.

"Oh shit, suck it bitch! Take all of this dick!"

Knowing that he was close to exploding, I reached behind him squeezed his ass. I could feel his nuts tighten as they rubbed against my chin. Yep! My deep throating skills were just that potent! Feeling especially nasty because I knew I was being tapped, I decided to make a bold move. It was slightly risky but would pay off in a big way if I ever had to use it.

Slowly and purposely I inched my finger towards the crack of Professor Reynolds ass. When he didn't stop me, I proceeded to inch forward. I glanced up quickly and saw that his eyes were closed. He was in pure ecstasy. The blowjob I was giving him was blowing his mind. I have to admit too though, being filmed while I was sucking the Professor's dick was turning me on to no end. I had on a short blue jean skirt with no panties on.

It was a good thing to, because my pussy started running like a faucet. Simultaneously, I stuck my finger in his ass and sucked my jaws in as hard as I could. Professor Reynolds trembled at the feeling of the vacuum like pressure I had on his dick. Either he didn't feel my finger in his ass or didn't care. I then slowly started finger fucking him in the ass. At the same time he started pumping my mouth. I was so turned on, I could barely stand it.

Thick, milky cum dripped from my sex box and coated the floor. A few seconds later, I was moaning just as loudly as the Professor as he deposited babies into my belly a different kind of way. I came too as the sheer excitement of the lustful encounter had my whole body tingling. I was sure that Toi was having trouble holding the camera. If I knew her as well as I thought I did, she was probably fingering herself right about now. As the Professor's dick gradually deflated in my mouth, he jerked a couple more times. I knew from experience that this meant his dick was most likely extremely sensitive at this time. I locked my fingers behind his head and flicked the tip of his dick with my tongue. Professor Reynolds tried to pull away but I held firm.

"Oh God, wait, wait," he stammered as he put his hands on top of my head and tried to force me off of his meat. After a few more seconds, I took mercy on him and let him go. Professor Reynolds then leaned back into his chair with a satisfied smile on his face. His dick was still leaking cum as it lie next to his inner thigh.

It tasted so good, I had to seriously fight off the urge to put it back in my mouth and swallow the rest. For dramatic purposes only, I dragged my wrist across my mouth as if I were wiping off excess cum. Since I hadn't allowed any to escape my mouth, there was no need for me to do that. But it made a woman look nasty, something that all men loved.

"So," I began, as I walked around to the front of his desk and leaned on it. "We straight?" I asked.

Professor Reynolds stood up and pulled up his pants. He then took a deep breath and cleared his throat.

"What do you mean?" he asked with a slight smirk on his face.

My smile slowly disappeared.

"Excuse me?"

"I said what do you mean?" He repeated himself.

No this muthafucka ain't tryin' to play me! I looked towards the door again only to discover that Toi had left. I cursed myself silently for telling her to leave as soon as we got through so she wouldn't be in any danger of getting caught.

"I know damn well you not about to welch on a bitch! I thought we had a fuckin' understanding?"

"Ms. Robinson, I have no idea what you are talking about."

"Nigga, you know exactly what the fuck I'm talkin' about!"

"No, I really don't," he said calmly, as if his dick wasn't in my mouth just a few minutes ago.

I was heated. This little stunt he was trying to pull made me so glad that I had Toi tape the encounter.

"Oh hell nah! Nigga you shady as fuck! You know damn well that you said you would change my grade if I gave yo' ass some head!"

I was trying to give the nigga a chance to do right before I had to expose his ass. He would surely get fired if the tape ever got out.

"I said nothing of the sort young lady!"

Professor Reynolds then did something that made it personal. After leaning so close to me that I could smell his cologne, he whispered into my ear.

"However, if you would just bend over the desk so I can fuck the shit out of that pussy, I'll consider your proposal. Because I just love to fuck slutty students."

I felt like a fool! Here I was thinking that I was the one running shit and this nigga was playing me the whole time. Apparently I wasn't the first student to offer him some head or ass for a grade change. Truth be told, if he would've just bargained a little bit more instead of trying to strong arm his way into the pussy, I would have been more than willing to give it up. But since he wanted to try and fuck me over, I was gonna show him how a bitch like me got down. It was now time to up the ante.

"So, this how you want to play it, huh muthafucka?"

Professor Reynolds then opened his mouth to speak and paused. After looking around as if someone was going to hear him, he continued.

"Bitch, get the fuck out of my room before I throw your ass out."

Staring daggers at him all the way, I slowly walked towards the door.

"Oh, and just so you know. Your grade will remain an F until I get some of that pussy. It's Friday and since grades go in on Tuesday, that gives you the entire weekend to make your mind up. Have a nice day," he said, still smiling.

After walking out of the room, I slammed the door so hard, the window cracked. Although I had insurance against the kind of maneuver he was pulling, it was the way he was disrespecting me that had me fuming. When I got back to my dorm room, Toi was sitting at my desk with her legs propped up in the air smoking a cigarette. I forcefully pushed her legs onto the floor and dropped down onto my bed.

"Damn, bitch what the hell wrong with you?"

"How many times have I told you about putting your feet up on my desk?" I snapped.

Toi looked at me and cocked her head to the side. She knew that there had to something bothering me in order for me to go off on her like that. Her mouth then fell open ad she leaned forward.

"Oh hell no, girl, I know damn well that nigga didn't try to renege on y'all agreement?"

"Girl that's exactly what he tried to do!"

"That low down dirty muthafucka!" Toi shouted.

"Oh but that's not the worse part of it. After pretending like he didn't know what the hell I was talking about when I asked him about the grade change, that nigga had the nerve to talk to me like I was some trick ass bitch! And to top it off, he told me that my F would remain a fuckin' F until I gave him some pussy!"

"That's some trifling ass shit," Toi said, shaking her head from side to side. "That's alright though. When you show his ass this video, I bet you he changes his muthafuckin' tune then! That muthafucka don't wanna get fired so he gonna do whatever the fuck you tell him to do."

Toi then burst out into laughter. It slowly disappeared when she saw me shaking my head from side to side.

"What the fuck you shaking yo' head like that for?" She asked. "I know you gonna expose this muthafucka, right?"

"Toi, I have something much more devious in store for this nigga. The way he tried to play me, he's gonna have to pay a much steeper price. Instead of hurting him, I'm going to hurt someone he loves."

Toi looked at me confused. She had no idea what I meant and, for the moment, I wanted to keep it that way. I learned early in my life that you some things you had to just keep to yourself. Toi had no way of knowing that I'd been researching Professor Reynolds intensely for the last two weeks. I'd learned enough about his family to totally fuck him up for what he'd done to me. This nigga wanna play dirty? I'll show his ass how to play dirty.

Next Door Nympho 2

2
Candice

After tossing and turning for most of the night trying to think of evil shit to do to Professor Reynolds' bitch ass, my plan was pretty much formulated. I had almost fallen asleep when my alarm went off.

"What the fuck?" I mumbled groggily as I sat up in bed. "Why the fuck is the alarm set for Saturday?" I asked, knowing that Toi had to be the one to set the alarm since I hadn't.

"I knew yo' ass was gonna forget," she said as she walked back in from the bathroom. Being that she slept in the nude, her ass jiggled and her titties bounced. That was one of the many things that we had in common. Neither of us liked to sleep with our clothes on. I watched as her voluptuous frame carried her sexy package back to her side of the room. Now I've always been strictly dickly but if I ever did decide to test the other side of the sexual track, Toi wouldn't be a bad place to start.

"Forget what? Bitch, what the fuck are you talking about?"

"You were supposed to go with me to Cleveland today to visit my mom," she yelled from the other side of the room.

Oh Shit, I thought to myself. With the fiasco that had gone down with that dickhead, Professor Reynolds' yesterday, I had totally forgotten. A broad smile erupted across my sleep deprived face. I was always happy to ride with her to visit her mother and step-father. Except for my aunt, they were pretty much the only family I had.

My grandmother had passed away shortly after my mother was killed and living with my aunt was not at all what I'd expected. I thought we were going to bond and have the kind of relationship that I wanted to have so desperately with my mother but Aunt Charmaine turned out to be a recluse.

Not to mention that I was going through a rough time in my life and needed someone to talk to. But whenever I tried to talk to her about my troubling situation, she simply found an excuse to change the subject or ignored me altogether. For some reason a guilty look always appeared on her face when I would ask about the situation between my mother and Hank.

It best to let sleeping dogs lie, she would say. Despite the fact that I'd only spoken to her a handful of times since I'd enrolled at Kent State I did miss her. I slowly dragged myself out of the bed and stumbled to the bathroom. After the stress the Professor had put me through, I was more than ready to relieve some of it.

I hurriedly got out of bed and hopped in the shower. When I got out, Toi was sitting on her bed scrolling through her phone. If I had to guess I would have to say that the bitch was probably on face book. For some reason her ass loved to get on the social media and read about other people telling their business.

She'd even told a little of hers. Fuck that shit. The last thing I need is muthafuckas desperate for some news to be all up in my shit. I went in the closet and pulled out a tight black dress that came to my thigh. When Toi saw what I was about to put on, she frowned.

"Bitch, we ain't goin' to the fuckin' club. How come every time we go see my parents, you gotta dress like you tryin' to catch a fuckin' man and shit?"

"Bitch, please. Don't hate me 'cause I look good. I'm the shit and you fucking know it."

"Whatever, hoe. More like a piece of it," she cracked.

Toi stood up and stretched. She was at least two inches taller than I was and sometimes I felt a tad intimidated. But whenever I started feeling that way, I just reminded myself that I was Candice fucking Robinson. Ain't a bitch alive got shit on me. I'd be lying if I said that Toi wasn't sexy as hell though. Her five foot eight inch frame carried her package well. Her bronze colored skin was naturally shiny and had a fluorescent glow to it. And although her hair was shorter than mine, stopping just below the middle of the back of her neck, it was full of life.

And those eyes! Oh my God, those eyes! They were light grey and made Toi look amazingly exotic. I don't know why but every time I look at them, I get the strange feeling that I've seen them somewhere before. I know that sounds crazy, but it's true. The way she used to stare at me had me thinking that she was bi-sexual. Every now and then I would look up and see her staring at me with the strangest smirk on her face that I had ever seen in my life.

"You ready to go, broad?" She asked.

"Let's roll," I shot back.

Both of us grabbed our purses and headed out the door. We both looked like bona fide models as we strutted towards the elevator. A couple of wanna-be dime pieces were in the hallway running off at the mouth as we passed. It was no secret that Toi and I were both despised by almost every other girl in the dorm. Whether it was because of our good looks, sassy attitudes, or the sheer ability to take one of these bitches men whenever we felt like it, these hoes were stuck in serious hate mode. Jealous bitches.

"Oh shit, I forgot something," Toi said just before we got on the elevator.

"Go 'head to the car and I'll be there in a second."

Shrugging my shoulders I hopped on the elevator and pressed down.

"Make sure you lock our door. I'd hate to have to fuck one of these sideline hoes up for stealing our shit," I yelled out just before the doors closed. I heard one of them bitches pop their lips but that's all they better do. After getting off the elevator, I suddenly realized that I couldn't get in the car because Toi still had the keys.

"Fuck!" I cursed to myself as I headed for the exit. When I got outside, there was a slight chill in the air, causing me to shiver. Quickly and gracefully I walked towards Toi's silver Acura. I leaned against the car and waited for her, all the while looking like the fine bitch that I was. All of a sudden, my ears started to ache. A voice that I'd been desperately trying to get away from pierced my eardrums.

"Hey Candice, can I holla at you for a minute?"

A migraine ensued as I closed my eyes and rubbed my temples. Before I even opened them back up, I knew exactly who I would see.

"Byron, what the fuck do you want?"

Byron was one of my former fuck buddies. We started messing around about three months ago. It was all good until this nigga started catching feelings. That shit pissed me off, 'cause I told his ass from the jump that I wasn't looking for any kind of serious relationship. I should have known after the way his ass wanted to cuddle after the first time I let him hit it that he was gonna be a fuckin' problem.

After the stupid muthafucka had the nerve to introduce his mother to me, I cut his clingy ass off quick. The last thing I needed was for this lame ass nigga or his mother to start planning wedding bells. Fuck that shit! All I wanted to do was grab a meal or two and screw.

"Byron what the fuck do you want?"

Byron stopped about ten feet in front of me. He looked from left to right to see if anyone had heard me. He was obviously embarrassed by my tone.

"Yo' why the hell you gotta talk to me like that Candice?"

"Nigga, 'cause I'm tired of you buggin' the shit outta me! Can't you take a hint? Leave me the fuck alone!" I yelled.

At this point, I didn't give a shit who heard me. This muthafucka was tap dancing on my last nerve and it was time to set his ass straight once and for all.

"You know Candice, that's some real ratchet ass shit to say! I mean after you done met my moms and shit, you gonna just dis a nigga like that?"

"Met your moms? Nigga, I didn't ask to meet your damn mother! That was yo' silly ass idea! You tricked me into that bullshit! Look, Byron! We had a few good times but now it's over! Done! Leave me the fuck alone!"

Byron's eyes watered. *'Look at this weak ass nigga'*, I thought to myself. *'I need to bottle this pussy and sell it for profit.'*

"Well, can we at least be friends?" He asked shamelessly

I just stared at his goofy ass. He just didn't want to take no for an answer.

"Byron, you know damn well we can't be friends. That shit would never work."

Suddenly, Byron's whole demeanor changed. He went from wounded bird to angry lion. His nostrils flared and his breathing got heavier.

"Oh, so you think you gonna just throw a nigga out like some garbage, huh? Bitch you must don't know who the fuck I am!"

Byron flexed his thick muscles and gritted his teeth. He had me scared shitless but I wasn't about to show any fear.

"Nigga, I know just who the fuck you are! A fuckin' bench warmer for the football team! Now get the fuck outta my face!"

The look on Byron's face prompted me to start reaching inside my purse for the straight razor that I carried. But before I could complete the task, Byron grabbed my wrists and started shaking me.

"Bitch, don't you ever talk to me like that!" Byron's brute strength caused my brain to rattle. Spit flew from his mouth and landed on the bridge of my nose as he rained insults on me.

"Nigga get the fuck off of me!" I screamed as I tried to break free of his grip.

"Aye yo,' what the fuck is going on out here?" Toi blurted out.

I'd never been so glad to see someone in my life. Byron stopped shaking me long enough to turn around and stare daggers at Toi.

"None of ya' muthafuckin' business! Kick rocks hoe!"

Byron then turned his attention back to me.

"Bitch, I'ma teach you how to respect a real nigga like me!"

Byron then lifted his hand in the air, preparing to slap the taste out of my mouth. In a desperate move to avoid being assaulted, I knee'd him in the balls as hard as I could.

"Ow shit!" He screamed as he doubled over in pain.

While he was momentarily incapacitated, I opened the door on the passenger's side and quickly jumped in. I was more than ready to get the fuck outta dodge. Toi must've been thinking the same thing, because before I could say a word, she was in the driver's seat sticking the key in the ignition. We had to get away from this crazy ass muthafucka. As fast as she could, she put the car in gear and pulled off, leaving Byron in the parking lot holding his nuts.

# # #

My blood pressure was still on the rise as we hit the highway. I couldn't believe that punk ass nigga had the nerve to put his fuckin' hands on me. Now I have two muthafuckas on my shit list. I looked over at Toi, who hadn't said a word since we got in the car, and sighed. She cut her eyes towards me and quickly twisted her lips. She knew exactly what I was thinking.

"Go ahead girl. Blaze up," she said, knowing that I needed some calm down. Even though Toi was a weed head too, she rarely allowed smoking in her ride. But this qualified as a special occasion. That nigga had me fucked up if he thought he was just going to put his hands on me and I was just going to forget about it. I had a trick or two up my sleeve that no one even knew about yet. When you have good pussy, you always have an ace in the hole.

The farther I got away from Byron, the better I felt. After firing up the blunt I had in my purse, I let the window halfway down. I inhaled it deeply, held it in my lungs for what seemed like an eternity, and blew it put of the window. I instantly felt better. Time seemed to fly by and before we knew it, we were pulling into the driveway of her parent's home.

    Before we could even get out of the car good, the front door was opening and Mr. and Mrs. Hawkins were coming out on the porch. Both of them had warm smiles and welcomed us with open arms. After the bullshit I'd been through the last twenty-four hours, I welcomed this weekend get-a-way.

3
Candice

Like they always had before, Toi's parents made me feel right at home. As soon as I walked through the door, the smell of food invaded my nostrils. If my sense of smell was correct, and it usually was, Sausage, Pancakes, French toast, and Scrambled Eggs were about to be devoured. Sensing that I hadn't eaten anything that morning, my stomach growled like a wolf.

"I know y'all probably starving so y'all better come and get some of this good food."

"Can't nobody cook like you baby," Mr. Hawkins said, in search of a few brownie points. Mrs. Hawkins blushed at her husband's compliment but blushed even more when he slapped her on the ass.

"Please, Javis, not in front of the kids."

"Kids? Cathy, those are grown ass women," he laughed.

"Whatever," she said as she walked up to Toi and gave her a hug. "She'll always be my baby."

For some reason, the embrace looked awkward to me. Like they were doing it for my benefit, although I don't know why the hell they would do that.

"Okay, people. Let's go eat," Javis suggested.

He didn't have to tell me twice. Strangely, Toi wasn't saying anything, but I was too hungry to give a damn. After smashing my first helping of food, I greedily asked for seconds.

"Damn bitch, save some for someone else," Toi mumbled, while elbowing me in the side. I gave her the finger and kept right on eating. As we ate, Toi's parents informed both of us that they had each taken the day off.

They wanted to spend the weekend showing us a good time, so they decided to kick it off by taking us to the movies. I really didn't like going to matinees, but since they were paying, I figured fuck it. After Toi's mom cleaned off the table, we all just sat around bull shitting until it was time for us to go. Javis had already bought the tickets, so we didn't have to wait in line, although when we got there, there weren't that many people in line to begin with.

"Y'all girls get some popcorn and meet us inside," Cathy said. Javis then gave us our tickets and the two of them went into the theatre.

"Okay. At some point we're gonna have to ditch they old asses and have some real fun," Toi said, smiling at me wickedly. My dick antennae immediately went up. My eyebrows raised as I asked her what she had in mind.

"Well, a couple of high school friends of mine want to hook up tomorrow night. I've already set that shit up girl."

"Oh yeah? How they look?" I asked, "'Cause I can't be seen with no ugly muthafucka."

They look alright," she said, shrugging her shoulders. "And it ain't like you marrying the muthafucka bitch you just going out to have a little fun. Shit, you acting like you better than he is already."

"I don't have to be marrying him to want his ass to look good," I responded dryly. "And I am better than his ass."

"Whatever, hoe. You always…"

As we got to the counter, Toi stopped talking in mid-sentence. Her eyes narrowed into tiny slits. With a confused look on my face, I followed Toi's gaze and saw that it had landed on a petite, dark skinned chick sporting a nappy weave. The girl behind the counter stared right back at Toi. I didn't know what the fuck was going on, but it didn't take a genius to know that these two hoes didn't like each other. The girl behind the counter folded her arms defiantly.

"What you want, bitch?" She asked Toi.

"I wanna piss on your grave, but since your ass is still alive I guess that's not going to happen right now. Give me a large tub of popcorn and 2 large Sprites."

"Oh, you wanna be a smart ass? Fuck you then, I'm on break!"

"Break? Bitch, please! Do your fuckin' job!"

Hearing the commotion, a thin man with a short afro came sprinting over. He had on a blue blazer and a tie, so I figured that he was a manager.

"Hey, hey what's going on over here?" He asked with concern in his voice.

"This rude little heifer won't take my order," Toi shouted.

"What? Vanessa, go stand over there and wait for me."

"But she…"

"Go stand over there!"

The worker stomped off in a huff. Toi could barely contain the smirk on her lips. The manager then turned back to Toi and started apologizing his ass off. It took everything in me not to bust a gut laughing.

"Ma'am I am so sorry about the cashier's poor attitude. I can assure you that she will be disciplined for this. Please accept the popcorn and drinks on us."

"Yeah, okay. But you need to do something about her rude ass! I especially didn't like the way she was picking her nose when we walked up," Toi lied on the girl.

This bitch was treacherous. I was going to have to keep my good eye on her ass. The manager's mouth fell open. He looked at Vanessa with disdain and slowly nodded his head. I knew right then that this would be her last day working there. As we walked back to the theatre, Toi giggled sinisterly.

"Tramp ass bitch."

"Damn, what the fuck was that all about?" I asked.

"Girl, it's a long ass story. I just hate that fuckin' bitch. The only person I hate more than that hoe is…you know what? Let's just go back in here and watch this damn movie. Fuckin' slut done drove my blood pressure up." When we got back inside, Toi's parents were frowning at us.

"Damn, did they have to plant the damn popcorn seeds?" Javis asked, snatching the tub out of her hand. Toi just glared at him as she slid by her parents on the way to her seat. An empty seat was left on the end next to the aisle and I was more than happy to sit in it. When Toi looked back and saw that I wasn't following her, she held her palms up as if to ask why I wasn't coming to sit next to her.

I pretended that I didn't see her as I got comfortable in my seat. Seconds later I received a text from her asking me why I wasn't sitting next to her. I texted back a lie, telling her that I sat on the end just in case I had to go to the bathroom because I didn't like to scoot by people. I had my reasons for sitting where I sat but I wasn't going to tell her what they were.

It was none of her fuckin' business. I then went to the draft section of my phone and sent out the text message that I had already pre-typed. *'I'ma suck every drop of cum outta that dick tonight,'* the message read. Seconds later, Cathy elbowed Javis in the shoulder.

"Turn that damn cell phone off," she whispered in his ear.

Javis reached down and snatched it off of his hip. Even in the darkness of the theatre, I could see the smile on his face. I took a glance at Cathy and saw that she was deeply into the movie, so I eased my hand into her husband's lap and grabbed his dick giving it a gentle squeeze. Little did Cathy or Toi know, I had been sampling Javis' meat for some time now. As I suspected, it had gotten rock hard. I could almost taste the salty head sliding in between my lips.

That nigga loved it when I gave his ass head. But as much as he loved having his dick sucked, he loved smashing this sweet pussy even more. Add that to the fact that I let him fuck me in the ass, something that his wife would never let him do, there is no wonder he keeps coming back for more. Sprung had his ass sprung.

Next Door Nympho 2

4

Charmaine

Although the sun was shining, the chill still cut through my bones like a knife through butter. The September wind seemed angry this afternoon as it howled in the swirling air. Guilt held my soul in a bear hug and refused to let it go. Even after I had gotten down on my knees and begged the Lord for forgiveness, it still held tight. They say the eyes are the windows to the soul. Well, aside from the fact that I look damn good in them, that's one of the reasons that I wear shades.

As I slowly walked up to my mother's tombstone, the pressure in my chest increased. It's the same way every year. When I first started visiting her grave, I thought I was having a heart attack when this first happened. But I came to find out that it was an anxiety attack instead. My doctor prescribed me some medication, even though I told him that I only have this attack one day out of the year. Unfortunately, today was that day.

I struggled heavily to hold back the tears that were destined to free themselves as I knelt down in front of my mother's tombstone and wiped off some dirt that had settled there. Before I even knew what was going on, my emotions poured out and I burst into tears. Seeing that this had never happened before, I was now certain that the guilt was getting to me. There was so much that I wanted to tell my mother.

There were so many things that I wanted to discuss with her. So many things that I had to tell her. Well, one thing in particular. And maybe if I would have told her, it would have given her the strength and will to survive after her stroke. Towards the end, it seemed like she just gave up and I ask myself everyday if she had known that she had two grandchildren instead of one would it have made a difference in her recovery.

"I'm sorry, mama," I mumbled to the grave as if she could hear me.

After standing there for thirty minutes, thinking and crying, I turned to my right and walked to the second reason for my despair. My sister Diamond. Even though she was a bona fide bitch and a certified hoe, she too deserved to know the truth. But as bad as I felt about deceiving her, I had no tears for Diamond. The way she treated Candice was a disgrace.

Her daughter deserved a better child hood than the one Diamond gave her. I am so worried about Candice. She seems to be following in her footsteps. I only hope and pray that she grows out of it. A few drops of rain interrupted my thoughts and slapped me on the bridge of my nose. Looking up in the sky, I saw dark clouds circling. It was clear that the skies were getting ready to open up and unleash something nasty on the Cleveland streets.

Hurriedly, I scampered back to my car and hopped in. My mother died without me telling her that she had another granddaughter. My sister died because of a lie. I can't go through this again. No more deceptions. No more lies. Candice is all I have. I have to tell her the truth and let the chips fall. What will be, will be.

5
Candice

Slowly and quietly, I crawled out of the bed. Shivering as soon as my bare feet hit the floor, I quickly grabbed my socks. It was cold as fuck in the Hawkins' guest room. I wondered silently how many nights Javis had frozen his balls off in this very room. In my mind there had to be quite a few occasions when he got pissed off and stormed out of their bedroom because she wouldn't give up the pussy.

I quickly slipped into the slippers that I'd left there during me and Toi's previous visit and headed for the door. After lying awake in this ice box they call a room for the last couple of hours, I was ready for hot action. Me and Toi had hit the liquor store earlier and, judging from the amount of vodka she'd consumed, I knew that she would more than likely be knocked out for the entire night. Javis had told me not to worry about his wife, because he was going to slip a crushed sleeping pill into her drink.

Low down muthafucka. But that was Cathy's problem. All I wanted was the dick. Plus the old nigga paid good. I didn't start off planning to get paid. The shit just happened. After riding him like the lone ranger rides silver one night, he gave me two hundred dollars and told me use it for things I needed at school. It's not that I'm trying to hurt Cathy. She's a cool lady. She just seems like a boring bitch. I bet she doesn't even suck his dick. And if she does, I'm positive she doesn't swallow.

Shit, I love the taste of cum going down my throat. That's why I charge his ass extra whenever he wants to cum in my face. I'd rather have it in my belly. I heard somewhere that semen is good for your skin, but I think that shit is just a myth. Easing my way out of the bedroom, I shook my head as I passed Toi's bedroom and her drunken ass snoring loudly. I'd purposely allowed her to consume more than me so I wouldn't be fucked up to the point that I couldn't get any dick. I then tip-toed down the stairs and headed for the kitchen. Sneakily, I headed for the door on the other side of the room, which led to an attached garaged.

It wouldn't be the first time we fucked in the back of Javis' conversion van and it certainly wouldn't be the last. I eased the door open and slid my thick frame into the garage. It was cold in there too, but what I planned on doing was going to heat that bitch up in hurry. Walking up to the van's door as quietly as I could, I reached for the door handle and jumped back slightly startled when it opened.

"Damn, nigga, you almost scared me to death," I whispered.

"You know you don't have to be scared of me baby girl. Come on in here and let daddy play in that pussy."

"What makes you think I want you to play in my pussy?" I asked sassily.

"Quit playing girl. You know you want big daddy up in that coochie."

Lustfully, I licked my lips as Javis stroked his member. It stuck out of his silk navy-blue boxers like a harpoon. My pussy started to throb as I climbed in, preparing to get a taste of Moby dick. With my eyes on the prize, I crawled between Javis' legs. As I lowered my head down, Javis jumped as I teased him with my tongue, flicking it back and forth across the head of his dick.

"You like that shit, don't you daddy?" I asked seductively.

"Oh, shit, baby, you know I like that shit. Stop teasing daddy, girl. Put it in your mouth."

Obeying his command, I opened my mouth wide and let his snake slither down my throat. He couldn't help but moan loudly as I worked my magic. I didn't have to look back to know that his toes were curling in his socks. When it came to giving head, I was the bomb.com.

Javis then grabbed both sides of my face and began fucking me in the mouth. I could taste the pre-cum leaking out of the tip. I increased the suction in my mouth and it drove him wild. Once I started deep-throating him, I felt his balls start to tighten. This nigga was getting ready to cum. Fuck that shit. I wanted to get fucked. The last thing I wanted was for him to bust and to have to wait to wait thirty minutes for him to get hard again.

"What the fuck?" He asked, when I stopped abruptly. Without saying a word, I turned around and got on my knees. Although it was difficult to maneuver inside the van, I was determined to get fucked doggy style. After looking back at him, I gave Javis a wicked grin.

"Come on daddy. Get this pussy," I purred. I didn't have to tell Javis twice. It took him all of two seconds to get up on his knees and mount me from behind. I could tell that he was ready to smash the pussy by the way he roughly shoved his meat into my cum canal.

"Oh, shit," I yelled lightly. I wasn't' used to Javis man-handling me so quickly. Usually he would start off slow. But this time he just slammed his cock inside and started ramming my cunt. I gotta admit though, I was loving the shit! It turned me on to no end!

As he grabbed my hips and pumped into me like a jackhammer, I threw it right back at his ass. The windows were already starting to steam up from our heavy breathing and the heat induced by our bodies. The van rocked in rhythm as we went at it like two wild beasts.

"Oh, yes, baby, give it to me," I moaned in ecstasy. The sound of his balls slapping up against my ass was music to my ears. The only thing that sounded sweeter was the nasty talk and grunts we were engaged in. The sweat from Javis' face splashed onto my back as his grip tightened around my waist.

"Harder, daddy! Fuck this pussy harder!" I hollered.

Javis responded to the challenge like a man half his age. With his left hand still clutching my hip, Javis raised his right hand and slapped me across the ass. The stinging sensation made my pussy even wetter than it already was. Javis then reached forward and grabbed a handful of my hair. Simultaneously, he pulled my locks and pumped his javelin in even deeper. I know it sounds borderline crazy but I wanted him to hurt the pussy! I wanted to feel pain! I wanted to feel his dick touching my spine! Shit, if I wasn't walking funny afterwards then it wasn't a good fuck to me.

"That's it daddy! That's the way I like it! Pound that shit, baby! Kill that muthafuckin' pu…"

I stopped in mid-sentence when I didn't hear Javis pumping me anymore. Looking back at him, my face turned into a mask of anger. He had taken his member out and had begun stroking it.

"The fuck you doin'? Put that muthafucka back…Oh fuck!" I yelled when he stuck it back in my hole. But this time, it wasn't the cum hole, it was the shit hole. I should have known that he was gonna want to fuck me in the ass.

"Oh God!" I screamed as his dick traveled through my rectum. Still wanting all of it, I laid my head on the arm rest, reached behind me, grabbed my ass cheeks, and spread them as wide as I could in order to give him more entry room. Seeing both of my hands, Javis took advantage and grabbed both of my wrists. He then pulled and pumped at the same time.

His nuts tightened, letting me know that he was getting ready to blow. I thought about asking him to cum in my mouth but decided that I didn't want to taste my own ass hole. Instead I told him that I wanted him to cum on my ass.

With one loud grunt, Javis pulled out and squirted sex juice on top of my booty. He then swept his dick back and forth across my ass, rubbing it in like lotion. The cum that wasn't rubbed in ran down the crack of my ass and tickled the bottom of my pussy lips. Javis then told me to turn on my back and spread my legs.

"Your turn, baby girl," he said, diving head first into my patch.

As hot and horny as I was, I didn't take long to drench his chin with my love. A satisfied smile erupted onto my face as I panted with pleasure.

"Come on baby," Javis said, pulling me up. "We better get the fuck outta here before Toi or Cathy catches us."

The cum that was on my night gown stuck to my ass as Javis helped me out of the van. As we headed back towards the kitchen door, the sight of Cathy's .38 pointed directly at our heads stopped us in our tracks.

Next Door Nympho 2

6

<u>Unknown</u>

A sinister smile crossed my face as evil thoughts ran through my mind. I would love to take a cordless drill, stick it in Candice's ear, and push it clean through to the other side. Then I would pray that God would keep her alive so that I could pour a bucket of alcohol into the drilled hole. As you can probably tell by now, I hate this bitch.

Through no fault of her own, I despise her ass. If it wasn't for that slut of a mother of hers…well, let's just say that I'd be a much happier person. That bitch infected someone I loved with HIV and since I can't exact my revenge on her dead, rotten pussy having ass, I'll settle for her daughter. They say revenge is a dish best served cold.

Well, the dish that I'm preparing for her ass is gonna taste like a bowl of snow in December. I also wouldn't mind feeding that bitch Chamaine some oatmeal with glass in it. I know Diamond was her friend, but I can't understand how she could let this shit ride. Regardless of our situation, she'd better not get in my fuckin' way or I'll put her out of her misery as well. But Candice has to suffer. She has to know what it feels like to have your life slipping away from you and not being able to do anything about it.

Yes, I'm alive and well. But a person that I had a lot of love for in my heart for is gone. Again, I know that this is not her fault. But the bitch is guilty by association. From what I've heard, Candice's mother, Diamond, was one of the biggest sluts in Cleveland. I guess the apple doesn't fall far from the tree. With tears stinging my eyes, I reached into my pants pocket and pulled two pictures.

Placing one in each hand, I stared at one for a few seconds and then at the other. The one in my left hand disgusted me so much; I hocked and spat on it, while the one in my right hand found its way to my lips for a gentle kiss. With swirling emotions tugging at my heart, I stared at them both. I hate one. I love the other. The funny thing about it is…I've never met either one of them.

7
Candice

A light stream of piss ran down my leg as I stared down the barrel of Cathy's pistol. Finding myself on the business end of a gun was not how I envisioned spending my weekend. I guess me and Javis had gotten so wrapped up in screwing that we hadn't realized how much noise we were making. Apparently it was enough to wake Cathy from her sleep.

I glanced over at Javis, who was just standing there with his mouth hanging open. He was frozen with fear. When I looked back at Cathy, her eyes revealed pure hatred. Her finger trembled on the trigger. I was scared shitless. I didn't know whether to run, cry, or beg for my life. But whatever I was going to do, I had better do it fast. Cathy looked like she was about to lose it.

"Did you two sneaky muthafuckas think y'all could fuck around behind my back and I wouldn't find out?" Cathy spat.

"Cathy, hold up. I…"

"Nigga, shut the fuck up!" She said as she cocked the pistol. "Both of you sneaky muthafuckas, get the fuck downstairs in the basement!"

Slowly and fearfully, we walked towards the basement steps. Fear gripped my body as Cathy continued to point the gun at us while leading us down into the basement. I looked back at Cathy, who had on a short, sheer, pink colored negligee and a chill ran down my spine.

The dark look in her eyes told me that she was planning to do some serious bodily harm to both of us. I jumped as she slammed the door behind us. I was so startled; I almost tripped and fell to the floor. Javis reached and tried to catch me but his wife's cold voice stopped him in his tracks.

"Let that slut fall!" She said.

Their basement was nice. It looked better than most people's living rooms, with wall to wall beige carpet, leather Italian furniture, and freshly painted walls. In the corner rested a refrigerator. A pool table sat in the middle of the floor. Cathy then lifted her foot and kicked Javis in his ass.

If I wasn't in the predicament that I was in, I would have cracked up laughing at his ass. I took another look at Cathy and, for the first time since I'd known her, saw her real beauty. She may have acted like an airhead at times, but the bitch was gorgeous. I could see her nipples poking out through her negligee. They looked hard and perky.

If it wasn't for the crazy ass look in her eyes, I would think she was turned on. I looked back at Javis, who had lost his balance and fallen over onto the couch and thought to myself, this is not good at all. I would give anything for Toi to wake up, come downstairs, and talk some sense into her mother.

"So I can't satisfy you huh? You want to fuck this tramp behind my back, huh?"

Cathy held the gun firmly, as she walked over to me and pointed it at my chest. I was sure that at any minute I was going to piss all over myself.

"Stand over there bitch," she said pointing to where the pool table was. Not wanting to get shot, I did exactly as I was told. Cathy then walked over to her husband, who was now sitting on the couch and turned her back to him. She then lifted up her negligee and bent over.

"Do what you do best, muthafucka!"

A sly smile formed on Javis' face as he reached up and grabbed Cathy's ass cheeks. Cathy let out a light moan as Javis parted her ass and stuck his tongue deep into the crevice. I stood there speechless as Cathy reached between her legs and started fingering herself. Javis' dick got rock hard, listening to his wife squeal with pleasure. After getting her salad tossed for a few minutes, Cathy threw the gun on the couch and began pinching her nipple. Javis had now started stroking his dick.

"Is it hard yet, baby?" Cathy asked him.

"Yep. Come get this muthafucka."

Cathy then crawled up on the couch and lowered her head onto Javis' meat. With my mouth still open, I continued to stare. It wasn't until that very moment that it hit me. This was a fuckin' set-up. These two perverted ass muthafuckas had planned this shit. Not that I was complaining, mind you. Fire shot through my body as I stared at Cathy's head bobbing up and down on Javis' meat. Cathy then shot me an inviting look.

"Are you just gonna stand there bitch, or are you gonna come over here and help me suck my husband's dick?"

She didn't have to ask me twice. As fast as I could, I moved towards the couch and got down on my knees. The cold floor sent shivers through my spine but I ignored it and concentrated on the task at hand. I was extremely aroused as I licked one side of Javis' shaft while Cathy licked the other. I was just getting into it, when Cathy suddenly grabbed a handful of my hair and yanked my head.

Then, before I could stop her, she jammed her tongue in my mouth and gave me the wettest tongue kiss

I'd ever had in my life. I was shocked. But what freaked me out the most was that I actually found myself enjoying it. Her lips were soft and juicy. I jumped as I felt a finger snake its way up inside my now wet cunt.

Javis hands were on top of our heads so I knew it had to be Cathy who was fingering me. Then she abruptly stopped kissing me and stared into my eyes. With a naughty look in her eyes, she licked her lips and smiled.

"Baby, I wanna see you fuck this bitch," she said to her husband. "But first," she said, looking back at me, "I hear you got some good tasting pussy. You mind if sample it?"

Without waiting for a response, Cathy helped me to my feet and sat me down on the couch. She then spread my legs wide and got on her knees. Cathy's eyes sparkled as she dipped her head down into my honey pot.

"Oh shit," I moaned and wrapped legs around Cathy's head. Her tongue darted in and out of my hole with speed and precision. I was on fire as she rolled it around my clit. I had never been with another woman before and I definitely wasn't a lesbian, but I have to admit, Cathy was giving me some of the best head that I'd ever had in my life. Instinctively, I grabbed the sides of her head and guided her deeper inside my sweet walls. Cathy the placed her palms on my inner knees and pushed my legs open as far as they would go. I was stretched to my limits.

"Open up bitch. Let mama in," she demanded.

Like an obedient child, I spread my thighs and allowed her entry into my sex cave. What she was doing to me was driving me absolutely crazy. Feeling left out, Javis started to pout.

"What about me?" He whined.

Glancing at his concrete hard member, I opened my mouth as wide as I could, letting him know just where he could put it. Javis was all too eager to stuff his dick into my mouth. The taste of it made me cum ever so slightly. Cathy must've really liked the taste of my love juice. As soon as it came out of me, she was swallowing as much of it as she could.

Just as I got ready to have a major orgasm, Cathy stopped, grabbed my arm, and yanked me up off the couch. Before I knew what was happening, she spun me around and pushed the back of my shoulder, forcing me to bend down. Javis then rubbed his dick against the back of my pussy. My leg trembled in anticipation of him sticking his golden rod into my hole.

"Stop teasing me nigga. Stick that pole in!" I yelled.

My back arched as Javis jammed himself inside of me. His balls slapped against my ass in perfect rhythm. At this point, I couldn't care less if Toi came downstairs and caught us. Hell, for as much fun as I was having, her ass could join in if she wanted.

As Javis pounded me from the back, Cathy climbed on the couch and got in front of me. Her pussy was directly in front of my face. There was no mistake as to what she wanted me to do. I looked at her pretty pussy and although I had never even smelled another woman's womb before, let alone tasted it, I had to admit, I was intrigued. I slowly inched my face forward as I prepared for my first taste of pussy.

"Stop stalling bitch! Eat that shit!" Cathy yelled at me.

When I didn't move as fast as she wanted me to, Cathy grabbed the back of my head and jammed my face into her muff.

"Eat it or suffocate, bitch, it doesn't make any difference to me!"

This bitch was off the chain. I had no idea that this ditzy acting broad had this type of dark side to her. Hesitantly, I stuck my tongue into the crack of her pussy and started licking her clit. From the way that her leg was shaking, I could tell that I was doing a good job.

It didn't take her long to cum in my mouth and for the first time in my life, I tasted the juices of another woman. I was on the verge of cumming myself as Javis continued to dig deep into my canal. With one mighty thrust, Javis emptied inside of me.

The hot feeling sent me over the edge as well. I was completely drained. My legs felt like jelly as I walked back up the stairs and made my way back to the guestroom. I could have sworn that I heard those two scheming ass freaks giggling as I walked across the kitchen floor.

8
Candice

I was so tired; I could barely hold my eyes open. Cathy and Javis' slick ass really put it on me last night. Here I was thinking that I was getting over by fucking Javis behind his wife's back and these two muthafuckas had set me up for a fuck-fest. We were all sitting at the table getting ready to have breakfast. Cathy walked in the room looking like Suzy homemaker, carrying a plate of sausages in one hand and a bowl of eggs in the other.

She sat them both down and made her way back into the kitchen. Her conservative attire belied the fact that she was an absolute freak-a-zoid in the bedroom. I was so tired that it took me a while to even notice that Javis had been rubbing my leg under the table. Apparently he got tired of waiting for me to respond, so he got up and went into the kitchen with his wife.

"The hell wrong with you?" Toi asked, elbowing me in the side.

She'd been looking at me funny from the moment we sat down to eat. I was starting to think that she'd heard me getting busy with her parents the previous night.

"Ain't shit wrong with me. And why the fuck do you keep looking at me like that?"

"Like what?"

"Like you pissed at me about something."

"I'm just wondering if your ass is gonna be able to go out tonight. You look like shit."

"Don't worry about me. I'll be more than ready."

Just then, Toi's parents came back into the dining room. Javis was carrying a large pitcher of Orange Juice while Cathy struggled with an oversized bowl of grits. She placed them on the table just as they were about to tip over.

"Damn, Cathy, you about to waste that shit all over the floor."

Cathy gave him a wicked scowl.

"Would you rather I wasted them in your face?"

"Yeah, yeah," Javis said, as he hunched up his shoulders and sat down at the table.

I ate my food as quickly as I could. After the night I'd had, all I wanted to do was lie back down in the bed and get some shut eye. Toi's spirits seemed to pick up after I told her that I was still going to kick it with her later.

"I don't feel too good," I told them. "I'm going back to bed."

I heard mumbles as I walked out of the kitchen, but I didn't give a fuck what was being said. All I wanted to do was take my tired ass back to sleep.

# # #

My head snapped up and jerked from side to side. Sweat poured from my forehead and dripped onto the bedspread. I'd just had the most disturbing dream I'd ever had in my life. I couldn't help but reach between my legs to see if my vagina was still attached to the bottom of my abdomen. Then I felt my chest to make sure that I still had a set of knockers.

The dream I'd had was downright sinister. Let me tell y'all about it. I was sitting in a bar by myself, having a few drinks when I was approached by a man with blotchy skin, bug eyes, and the worst haircut that I'd ever seen in my life. I had zero interest in this clown, but he sat down next to me and tried to mack any-fuckin'-way.

Although I didn't want to be bothered with his ass, he found it necessary to buy me several drinks. I know I was wrong for accepting them, but hey. The nigga was feeling generous, so I didn't want to be rude. But then the nigga started hinting that he wanted me to go home with him. That shit wasn't going to happen.

I was trying to find someone a little higher on the evolutionary chart. You know, someone with a few dollars in his pockets with a body like 50 cents, eyes like Michael Ealy, and a dick like Mr. Marcus. When the nigga started getting ignorant, I threw a drink in his face and headed towards the bathroom. Can you believe this muthafucka had the nerve to grab my arm, like I was his property or something.

I yelled at his dumb ass to get the fuck off of me and before I could really start cussing his ass out, the bouncer came over to see what the problem was. Liquor had this nigga talking ridiculous. It didn't seem like he was drunk to me, but when he jumped in the six foot-five two hundred and thirty pound bouncers face and started throwing insults at him, I knew this nigga had to be tipsy.

The bouncer proceeded to open up a serious can of whup-ass on him. He received a round of cheers when he picked the drunk up and tossed him out on the sidewalk. I thanked the bouncer, gave him my number, and asked him to call me the next day. For rescuing me, I'd already decided that a blowjob was going to be his reward. I stayed at the bar for another hour, but failed to come across anyone that was worth my time.

After leaving the bar, I hurried home so I could call up my annoying ass ex-boyfriend to see if he could come over and knock the dust off of my pussy. I really didn't want to be bothered with his clingy ass but my pussy needed some attention, and not the plastic kind. It needed some real meat. The closer I got to my apartment, the wetter my pussy got. My ex may have been annoying but he slung pipe like a porn star.

The only reason I didn't call him from my cell phone was because I wanted time to freshen up before he got there. I walked into my place of residence and kicked off my heels. The wine in the refrigerator seemed to be calling my name, even though I'd already consumed a large amount of vodka.

After pouring myself a glass, I downed it quickly and was ready for another. I refilled my glass and walked into my bedroom to set the scene and the mood. I flipped the switch on the wall and dropped the glass on the floor. It shattered upon impact, causing the wine to splash onto the bottom of the bedpost.

"Nigga what the fuck you doing in my apartment?" I yelled.

The pain in the ass from the bar looked up at me and smiled. He was stretched out in my bed with the sheets covering him from the waist down. Both of his hands were under the sheets and his right hand seemed to be moving up and down. It didn't take a genius to know that the nigga was stroking his meat.

"You need to stop acting like you don't want this dick. Come on over here and let me do some damage to that pussy."

For one brief second, I thought about taking him up on his offer. The liquor and wine had started talking to me and my pussy was on fire. But I still wanted to know how the fuck this asshole got into my apartment.

"I'm gonna ask you one more time. How the fuck did you get into my damn apartment?"

"Don't worry about how the fuck I got in here. You just better worry about the pounding I'm gonna put on that pussy."

I have to admit, he almost had me with that line. But then the nigga snatched the cover back and I almost choked on my own laughter. I don't know how the hell he thought he was going to pound on my pussy with his little three inch dick.

"Nigga what the fuck you think you gonna do with that little ass Vienna sausage? You couldn't fuck me in the ear and make me feel it with that mini-dick of yours."

I know I was wrong for laughing at him the way I was but I couldn't help it. This nigga was seriously lacking the cock department.

"Bitch, what the fuck you laughing at? I don't see a muthafuckin' thing funny!"

"Well, I do nigga! The shit I'm looking at between your legs is hella funny!"

Before I could get another snicker out, this psycho muthafucka was up on me. His right hand shot out and grabbed me by the throat so fast I didn't have time to react.

"Bitch who the fuck you think you talking to like that? Don't you know I will snap yo' gotdamn neck?"

Water welled up in my eyes. Desperately, I clawed at his hands and wrists in a vain attempt to get free. I wanted to scream but couldn't as his hands cut off any sound that threatened to get out. Out of sheer desperation, I knee'd him in the nuts.

"Shit! Bitch, I'm really gonna fuck you up now," he screamed as he released my neck and reached for his aching testicles.

Seeing my opportunity to get away, I sprinted through my bedroom door and ran straight for the front door. My heart was pounding like a drum. I didn't know why the fuck this was happening to me, but I was determine to make it out of this shit unscathed. Whatever this nigga was thinking about doing to me, he was going to have to catch me first. And as soon as I got out of my apartment, I was going to run across the street and call the cops on this crazy muthafucka.

I yanked open the door and pain immediately shot through my head. Whatever it was that slammed into my face damn near put my lights out. My ass hit the floor with a loud thud. I shook my head swiftly from side to side. I had to shake off the cobwebs and get the hell out of there. I was starting to feel like my life was in real danger. As my vision cleared, a familiar frame came into view. I blinked my eyes a few times just to make sure I was seeing what I thought I was.

It was the bouncer form the club, the one that had come to my rescue when I needed help at the bar. A loud laugh escaped his mouth a she reached down and yanked me up off of the floor. Still half dazed, I was powerless to stop him from taking me into the bedroom and dumping me on the bed.

"So, you like to knee muthafuckas in the balls, huh bitch?" The annoying man from the bar asked me.

He then took out a knife and put it between my legs. I don't know how or when it happened, but when I looked down I was completely naked from the waist down.

"So, you don't wanna give up no pussy huh, bitch? A'ight. I'ma make it so you can't give that shit to nobody!"

The bouncer grabbed me by the wrists and held me down on the bed. As much as I struggled, I just couldn't break free of his grip. Then, when I saw the knife that was in the man from the bar's hand go down and disappear, I knew I was done for. Oddly enough though, I didn't feel a drop of pain as he dug my insides out.

The bouncer laughed sinisterly as I was being mutilated. Blood covered the pain in the ass' wrists as he did surgery on my womb. I gasped as he held my bloody coochie in the air for me to see. Then, in one fell swoop, he swung the knife and chopped off my right breast. That was when I woke up petrified and in a cold sweat. So you can see why I'm checking myself to see if all of my womanly organs are intact.

Next Door Nympho 2

9
Candice

After getting over my nightmare, I started getting ready for the evening with Toi and the niggas she'd hooked us up with. I was going to beat her ass if this muthafucka turned out to be an asshole. I was going to torture her if he had a small dick. And I was going to absolutely kill her if this nigga's fuck skills weren't up to par. Even with the fucked up dream I'd had, the sleep did me a world of good. I was energized and ready for some hot action.

I quickly hopped in the shower and got clean while trying to decide if I wanted to ride the pole or get fucked doggy style tonight. I was determined to have a good time tonight because when I got back to Kent, I had major business to take care of. I was going to make Professor Reynold's bitch ass pay for playing me about my grade.

And I knew just what I was going to do to bring him to his ashy ass knees. But for the moment, I had dick to think about.

"Damn, bitch. Yo' ass ain't ready yet?" Toi asked as she stormed into the room. She'd been waiting on me for thirty minutes and looked quite annoyed because of it. "What the fuck is taking you so long?"

I ignored her for a few seconds before turning around and answering her question.

"You can't rush perfection," I said to her, just before applying my MAC lip gloss. I was dressed for some hot action, with a white mini-skirt hugging my hips and a cut off shirt that stopped just above my navel. To avoid having to take them off later, I decided to just not wear any panties at all. Toi, obviously trying to show off her figure as well, had a on a pair of skin tight Capri pants with a blouse that struggled to contain her breasts.

"Yeah, whatever. You ready to roll?" she asked.

"Let's do this," I answered after spraying a dash of perfume on my neck. After checking ourselves in the mirror one last time, we both headed downstairs. As we passed the living room, I glanced over and saw Cathy sitting in the recliner reading the bible.

"We out," Toi shouted.

"You girls be careful out there," Cathy said, sounding sincere. I honestly don't know if she said that just to be saying it or if she really meant it, but the look in her eyes had me thinking that she couldn't wait until we left so her and Javis could have a fuck-a-thon.

"We will," Toi assured her. She seemed to be oblivious to the fact that her mother was a freak. A nasty ass, dick sucking, pussy eating freak.

"The fellas are going to meet us there."

"Where the fuck is there?" I asked. It had just occurred to me that I didn't know where the hell we were going.

"We're meeting them at Denny's." My face immediately twisted up.

"Denny's? What the fuck kinda cheap ass niggas you hooking us up with?"

"Look Bitch. I told you that I would get you fucked. I didn't say shit about getting your ass treated to a five star restaurant. Don't start acting all sadity and shit."

As much as I wanted to cuss her ass out for talking to me like she'd lost her fucking mind, the bitch had a point. In my book, five star restaurants came second to a good hard dick any day.

"Just drive, bitch," was all I could think of to say.

The smirk Toi had on her face made me want to smack her ass. Glancing over at her briefly, I noticed for the first time that she wasn't wearing a bra. Her silver dollar sized nipples pushed against the fabric of her shirt. The sight of them caused my pussy to moisten.

I was beginning to wonder what the fuck was wrong with me. I'd always had a high sex drive, but that was for the dick. Now I was beginning to crave the cunt. It wasn't like I couldn't have stopped Cathy if I wanted to. I was just so damn curious about tasting pussy that it never crossed my mind to do so.

"The fuck you staring at me like that for?" Toi asked when she caught me ogling her tits.

"Huh?"

"I asked you what the hell you were staring at. I hope you ain't on that dyke shit, 'cause I'm strictly dickly baby."

"What? Girl, hell nah," I said, lying. "I'm just now noticing that yo' skanky ass ain't wearing no bra."

"So the fuck what? I bet your slutty ass ain't got no panties on," she shot back.

Before I could utter a response, the bitch shot her hand between my leg and up my skirt. Her middle and forefinger brushed against my pubic hairs.

"Hey, bitch! Cut that shit out!" I yelled although I secretly wanted her to slide them into my hole. Was I turning bi?

"Yeah, that's what I thought, bitch. Your ass can't hop on the dick fast enough." I laughed it off, hoping that she didn't notice that I had came slightly. Just her touch had caused my pussy to semi-release.

"Anyway," I said, changing the subject, "You never did tell me what the fuck this nigga looks like."

"Don't worry about all that. All you need to know is that he has a long, thick, dick."

My eyebrow arched up.

"And just how the fuck do you know?" I asked, folding my arms. It hadn't occurred to me that Toi might have been setting me up with her sloppy seconds. I wasn't going to turn the dick down, but the bitch could have at least told me if that was the case.

"I just know, alright? And no, I haven't fucked him, if that's what yo' ass is thinking."

That made me feel slightly better, although I was curious as to how she knew what the size of his penis was. Toi then pulled into the restaurant's parking lot, looked over at me, and winked.

"Let's go have some fun girl," she said, hopping out of the car. I was right behind her as we entered. I was hoping to see the dude that she'd hooked me up with before he had a chance to see me. I really don't know why. We women are just petty like that.

"Table for two?" the waitress asked.

"No thank you. We're meeting some friends here. I see them over there."

Toi then walked past the waitress before she had a chance to say a word. As we walked my eyes followed Toi's line of sight. When I saw the magnificent specimen that we were there to meet, my heart dropped. Sitting in a booth in the back were two of the finest men that I'd ever seen in my life.

One of them had a milk chocolate complexion with dark pool like eyes. He was the thicker of the two. His face was clean shaven and his front tooth was chipped but it was sexy to me. The other brother was two shades lighter with brush waves and a neatly trimmed goatee. Although he wasn't as muscular as his friend, he was by no means skinny. At that moment, I realized that it didn't matter which one of them I got. Either one of them could get the coochie.

"Damn, them niggas fine as fuck," I said excitedly.

"Yep, I know," Toi said, smiling.

"Which one of them is mine?" I was salivating at the thought of climbing in the sack with one of them. I honestly didn't care which one. Hell, as horny as I was, it could have been both of them.

"The dark skinned one is yours. The other one belongs to me," she said, possessively.

"Shit girl, that's fine with me. I'll take his chocolate ass any day of the week."

The closer we got to the booth, the wetter my pussy got. It was like it had a mind of its own when it came to sniffing out a dick.

"Sup fellas?"

"Sup girl," both of them spoke in unison.

Both of them then got up and hugged Toi so tight, I thought she was going to burst.

"I'm glad you didn't stand me up like you did the last time," said the one that Toi had already pegged as her date.

"Boy, don't start that bullshit. I told you that something important came up that day."

"Yeah, I bet," he said, giving her a sinister grin. "So, who's ya friend?" My date asked.

"Oh, my bad. This is my girl Candice."

"How you doing, pretty lady?"

The guy grabbed my hand and kissed it. I wasn't feeling that shit though. All I wanted from his ass is for him to put my ass in the buck. But for the sake of being polite, I played along.

"It's nice to meet you Candice. My name is Rashawn."

"It's nice to meet you too," I said as seductively as I could. It didn't take Rashawn long to start undressing me with his eyes.

"Hey Ms, lady. My name is Malcolm," Toi's date introduced himself.

"Nice to meet you too," I responded.

"How long have you been here?" Toi asked.

"About an hour and a half," Malcolm said.

After checking her watch, Toi popped her lips.

"Nigga stop lying! Yo' ass ain't been here no hour and a damn half!"

Both Malcolm and Rashawn started laughing.

"Yo' I'm just fuckin' wit' you. We only been here for like twenty minutes, tops."

"Twenty minutes?" Toi said, looking at her watch. "It's a quarter to nine now. we was supposed to meet here at eight o'clock, which means you mo fo's are late."

Malcolm looked at Toi like she was crazy.

"How the hell you gonna complain about us being twenty minutes late when yo' ass is damn near an hour late? Girl you betta go 'head on wit' that shit," Malcolm said, waving his hand at Toi dismissively.

"And plus," she said disregarding his last statement, "You niggas done started drinking without us."

Toi then snatched one of the bottles of Coronas off the table and started drinking out of it. Rashawn pointed at Malcolm and laughed out loud.

"Man I told you that she was gonna do that shit."

After drinking the last of Malcolm's beer, Toi sat the empty bottle down on the table.

"Girl, I done told you about that shit! I don't know where the fuck yo' lips been!"

Toi then leaned close to Malcolm and tried to whisper in his ear. I don't know if she wanted it to be a private comment or not, but I heard every word that she said.

"If you play your cards right, ain't no telling what part of your body my lips will end up on later tonight," she told him.

Malcolm jumped a little as Toi's hand dipped underneath the table. It didn't take a genius to figure out that she was probably squeezing his dick. In order to get our attention, the waitress, who apparently had been standing there the whole time, cleared her throat.

"Are you people ready to order now?" She asked with an attitude.

All four of our heads snapped around at once. You people? Who the fuck was this white bitch calling you people?

"Hell nah!" I said before I snapped before I could stop myself.

"And just what the hell you mean by you people?" Toi backed me up.

Seeing that she had struck a nerve, the redhead started backtracking. Holding up her hands in a defensive posture, the waitress, whose name was Suzie, tried to explain herself.

"I'm sorry. I didn't mean to offend anyone. I was just wondering if you guys were ready to order your food.

"Come back in ten minutes," Rashawn told her.

His voice dripped with anger. It turned me on. Hopefully, he would be taking his anger out on my pussy later on. After ten minutes, a different waitress came out. She too was Caucasian but had a much cheerier attitude than the previous one. She was also quite attractive.

As me and Toi ordered our food, the guys were openly staring at her. Toi didn't seem to notice, but I sure as hell did. I elbowed Rashawn in the side when I thought that he was staring at her a little too long. Rashawn looked at me with a twisted up expression on his face.

"Damn, ma what's up with the elbow?"

"Nigga please. You think I didn't see you looking at that bitch?" I said as if Rashawn was my man.

"Damn. A little possessive for a first date, ain't it?" He said smiling.

The fact that he was smiling told me that he wasn't pissed at me or turned off by my actions. That was good, because I damn sure didn't regret doing it. Hell, I'm Diamond Robinson's daughter. I don't play second fiddle to no bitch.

"I'm sorry boo," I said as if I felt bad. "It's just that you're so fucking fine, I don't want to share you with anybody tonight. I want you all to myself. I'm only going to be in town until tomorrow so I hope you can show me a good time."

The smile on Rashawn's face widened as I ran my hand up his thigh and let it come to rest just above his abdomen. I then ran my hand along the shaft. I was searching for the head. It was a little trick I used to find out how well a nigga was endowed. But this nigga was in a class by himself. It seemed like I would never get to the end. This muthafucka was hung like a horse. My pussy would be sore for days after letting this muthafucka smash it.

"Find what you're looking for?" Toi asked as she looked at me with a devilish grin. She knew exactly what I was doing. I guess two horny bitches really do think alike.

"Whatever, nosey ass bitch. Come to the bathroom with me right quick. I gotta ask you something."

Although Toi looked annoyed, she followed me anyway. The two of us got up and strutted across the floor. It was evident by the stares we got from some of the male customers that we were certified dime pieces. We were just about to enter the ladies room, when we heard someone calling our names. We turned around and looked directly in the faces of Javis and Cathy.

Me and Toi both looked at each other with confused looks on our faces. What the fuck were they doing here? Were they following us? When we left the house, Cathy looked like she was in for the night and Javis was nowhere to be seen.

"What the hell are they doing here?" Toi asked.

"Girl, how the hell should I know? They're you're fucking parents, not mine."

As we walked back towards the table where they were seated, I noticed Javis cutting his eyes at Malcolm and Rashawn. The look on his face screamed jealousy. *'I know this nigga ain't about to start tripping in here like I'm his woman or something,'* I thought to myself.

"Ok, I now y'all not following us," Toi said with a hint of attitude.

"No, we're not," he mother answered, matching Toi's tone. "We were going to order a pizza but changed our minds at the last minute, if that's okay with you."

Cathy was clearly annoyed at Toi's implication.

"Sorry," Toi said, throwing her hands up in a defensive posture.

"I see y'all got a couple of hot dates over there," Javis spoke up. Cathy elbowed him in the side.

"Javis mind your own business," she fussed.

"I am," he responded, staring straight at me.

'Oh, this muthafucka tripping for real,' I thought to myself. *'I ain't his bitch.'*

"Like you told me yesterday, those girls are grown. You two go ahead with your evening. we just called you over here to say hello," Cathy said, giving Javis a stern look.

"You think she's telling the truth about them showing up here being just a coincidence?" Toi asked.

"I don't know girl. She sounded legit but you know your parents better than I do. What do you think?"

The question lingered in the air like cigarette smoke as we headed to the ladies room. Toi never did give me an answer to my question. Her silence caused me to wonder.

10
Unknown

    Look at this bitch, strutting like she doesn't have a care in the world. She looks so much like her nasty ass mother, I want to throw up. Yeah, keep smiling bitch. Soon enough I will have my revenge. Then, after I'm done with you, I might just stop by the cemetery, drop my pants, and take a shit on your mother's grave.

    You two hoes are the definition of ratchet. Trying to stick to my plan has been hard as hell. The bitch may have some good pussy but that ain't gonna stop me from fucking her world up. Look at her! Just look at this slut! I want to stab her ass in the throat. Every time I think about the revenge I'm going to exact on her, I almost bust a nut.

    I know it's crazy but I even think about her ass when I'm fucking. My partner thinks that it's their sexual prowess that's rocking my world but in reality it's the thought of slitting this tramps throat. Now the bitch is smiling, showing all thirty-twos. Keep smiling bitch. Just keep smiling. Soon, you won't be able to.

Next Door Nympho 2

11

Candice

After leaving Denny's we went to Club 216 to get our dance on. Toi and I had followed the fellas there. When we arrived, we got out of Toi's whip and jumped into the SUV with our dates. Our eyes lit up at the sight of Rayshawn sitting in the passenger's seat puffing on a thick blunt. After taking three hits apiece we were all pretty blazed and ready to party. We all got out and started walking towards the entrance to the club. Because it was still kind of early, the line to get into the place wasn't that long.

"Sorry about that," Rashawn apologized after 'accidentally' touching my ass.

"Nigga please. You know damn well that you did that shit on purpose," I said smiling.

"Nah, ma, I'm a gentleman. You know I wouldn't do no shit like that," he said with a devilish grin on his face.

My pussy jumped as I looked down at the bulge in his pants.

"Hey, if y'all niggas coming in then come the hell on," the rude doorman yelled. We looked in front of us and saw that Toi and Malcolm had already gone inside. Rashawn mean mugged the doorman on the way in, but was paid no attention. The doorman simply re-attached the rope barricading the potential party goers back and stood there.

The music was loud and thumping, causing the windows to vibrate. It seemed as if any second they were going to break. The club had to be relatively new since I'd grown up in Cleveland and had never heard of it. Although I thought the name 'Club 216' was corny, the place did have a hint of elegance to it.

The maroon wall to wall carpet was thick and plush. The floor to ceiling windows were tinted so that the people inside could see out, but no one could see in. Rashawn looked like he was ready to hit the dance floor but my food hadn't had a chance to settle yet so his ass was just gonna have to wait.

"So what's good Toi? You ready to shake that ass or do you want to get a drink first?" Malcolm asked her over the music. Without answering his question, Toi headed straight for the bar.

"Man, I don't even know why you asked her that shit," Rashawn laughed. "You been knowing her long enough to know her ass was gonna wanna get a drink first."

The three of us then followed her to the bar. Me and Toi ordered Cosmopolitans while the fellas got straight vodka shots. After sipping on our drinks and conversing for about twenty minutes, we all smiled as the DJ put on a slow song. With the liquor heating up my insides, I grabbed Rashawn and pulled him onto the dance floor. The floor was a tad slippery and seemed like a lawsuit waiting to happen, in my opinion.

Toi and Malcolm followed us as we weaved our way through the crowd. The soulful sounds of Maxwell's song 'Fortunate' invaded my ears as I threw my arms around Rashawn's neck. I could tell that he was feeling it too the way he gripped my hips. Back and forth we swayed. With every second that passed, the sexual tension between us seemed to elevate. I was on fire. I thought I would lose it when Rashawn started licking and nibbling on my earlobe.

"Oooo, baby, that feels so good," I cooed. Rashawn's hands were strong yet gentle. They sensually caressed my hips and slowly dropped to my ass. I was ready to fuck right then and there as he palmed my juicy bottom. Rashawn then moved his right hand to the front of my body. His long fingers found the bottom of my skirt. With it being a mini-skirt, he had no problem reaching underneath it. I gasped slightly as he pushed his middle finger inside my wetness. I know I looked like a slut, getting finger fucked on the dance floor, but Rashawn's finger felt so good, I really didn't give a damn at the moment. Rashwan's finger probed and flicked my hot spots. The fact that his finger felt this good had me giddy as to what the dick must have felt like. Not wanting to be totally embarrassed, I tried hard to resist the urge to come, but this nigga was doing it to me. Just when I couldn't take anymore, the booming sounds of Usher's 'Yeah' blasted through the speakers, causing us both to jump and Rashawn's finger to slip out of my super moist womb.

"Ah shit," we heard people scream. Rashawn then went into a variety of dance moves. I looked over at Toi, who was looking back at me shaking her head. The wicked smile on her face told me that she'd seen it all. Malcolm tried to hide his smirk, but he too had probably seen the show. I gave both of them the finger and kicked my dance routine into high gear.

I'd always been a good dancer. Back in high school, I used to have niggas in line waiting to hit the floor with me. It had been a while but I still had my moves. I decided to show Rashawn just who he was dealing with. With a quick two step I had turned around and was backing that ass up on him. He was the most surprised person in the club when I started grinding my ass up against him. He fell off balance but quickly recovered.

I looked over at Toi again and saw that she was giving Malcolm all he could handle. The DJ played the song for what seemed like an hour. By the time he switched to another song, the four of us were drenched in sweat.

"Damn, I thought he was never gonna stop playing that song," Toi complained, as she plopped down on a stool at the bar. The place had gotten significantly more crowded since we'd come in so the tables that were unoccupied then were now taken.

"Y'all want another drink?" Malcolm asked.

"I would love another drink," I said, running my hand up Rashawn's leg. At the same time I said drink, I squeezed his dick, letting him know exactly what I was thirsty for. I was horny as fuck and didn't give a damn who knew it.

"I want another one too, but I don't want no fuckin' cosmo. I want what you're getting," Toi spat. Malcolm's forehead wrinkled.

"Baby girl, I'm about to get a shot of Jack…Straight!"

"And your point is what nigga?" she challenged. "Don't worry nigga," she said after a brief silence between the two. "I'm not gonna pass out and fuck up your chances of getting some pussy."

Malcolm tried to laugh it off, but the look on his face revealed that's exactly what he was thinking. Apparently the two of them had been through this scenario before. After the drinks were ordered, we gulped them down as fast as we could. Everyone seemed to be on the same page. We were all tipsy and ready for some hot action. Toi looked to be a little drunker than the rest of us as we made our way to the exit. On the way out, Rashawn purposely bumped into the doorman.

My heart stopped as the doorman balled up his fists and glared at Rashawn. From the looks of him, he seemed to be about six feet five inches tall and towered over Rashawn. He was also very muscular. The last thing I wanted was for Rashawn to get beat to a bloody pulp before he had a chance to give me some of his delicious meat.

"Come on baby, let's go," I pulled on Rashawn, trying to defuse the situation.

"That's a good idea sweetheart. You betta take his silly ass on before he ends up gettin' fucked up."

When Rashawn still didn't move, I whispered in his ear.

"Nigga do you want to smash some of this good pussy or do you want to stand here and argue with this fool all night?"

That did the trick. Rashawn followed behind me like a dog in heat. Toi and Malcolm, ten feet ahead of us by now, were groping each other shamelessly and were oblivious to what was about to go down. Toi then reached into her pants pockets and pulled out her car keys.

"Follow us," she said, tossing them to me.

"Where the hell are we going?" I asked.

"Bitch, stop asking so many questions. Just follow us," she said.

Malcolm laughed at her attempt to check me, which pissed me off. I made a mental note to tell her ass later about that shit. Me and Rashawn hopped in Toi's car and followed them out of the parking lot. It took a little less than ten minutes to get to our destination. During the ride over there, me and Rashawn made small talk. It was really unnecessary since I didn't want to get to know him like that.

All I wanted from his ass was a good roll in the hay. I did find out a few things though, like how the three of them knew each other. It turns out that they all went to high school together. Rashawn and Toi were friends first. A year later, they met Malcolm. They had just recently re-connected though. To my surprise, Rashawn said that he'd never played sports.

With his athletic build, I would have sworn that he was a football player. During the ride, Rashawn rubbed my shoulder. Smoothly and erotically, his hand fell to my breast. The minute his finger pinched my nipple, cum squirted from my hot pussy onto the seat. Yes, I was that hot and horny. Lucky for me, we had arrived. We pulled up in front of a nice looking colonial style house with a fence around it. We got out of the car and followed Toi and Malcolm into the gate and up the steps. Toi's drunk ass had to grab the rail to keep from falling on her ass. Apparently that straight shot of Jack Daniels she'd drank earlier had started taking control of her body.

"Damn baby, you aight?" Malcolm asked her.

Toi opened her mouth to speak but instead of words coming out of her throat, vomit came forth. She barely made it to the rail before barfing into the grass. She then staggered over to Malcolm, leaned up close to him, and tried to kiss him in the mouth. Malcolm quickly turned his head to the side, causing her lips to land on his jaw. Malcolm seemed annoyed as he pushed away and took out his keys to open the door. As soon as we got in the door, Toi ran through the house.

"Hey, you betta not throw up on my fuckin' toilet seat again," Malcolm yelled. "Drunk bitch," he mumbled. Although I didn't appreciate him talking about my girl like that, he was right. Her ass was tore the fuck up. Malcolm then walked over to his couch and plopped down. He seemed to be losing stem, but I could tell by the bulge in his pants that he still wanted to fuck. Hell, as fine as he was if Toi wasn't able to do anything with him tonight, I sure as fuck wouldn't mind having a threesome.

"The fuck y'all standing around for? Rashawn, you act like you ain't never been here before, nigga, sit yo' ass down."

Rashawn grabbed me by the hand and led me over to the opposite end of the couch. Just by the way he was touching me; I could tell that he couldn't wait to get into my pants. As soon as he sat down I dropped down onto his lap. I could feel his dick trying to push through his pants and find my vagina. Just then Toi came out of the bathroom looking like a rabid dog. Traces of vomit was in the corner of her mouth.

"Why the fuck is everyone so quiet? She asked. "I thought we was going to continue the party here."

"Girl, please. Yo' ass is wasted," Malcolm said.

Toi put her hands on her hips and shook her head. A devilish smile fell across her face. Switching her ass back and forth, she sashayed over and stood directly in front of Malcolm. Before any of us knew what was happening, she dropped to her knees and reached for Malcolm's zipper.

"Damn baby, what you doin' down there," he asked, smiling.

"Nigga, if you don't know what the fuck I'm doin', then I'm wit' the wrong muthafucka."

Toi pulled out his dick and stroked it gently. She looked at it with admiration as she lowered her head down onto the tip. Ever so slowly, she flicked her tongue back and forth across it. Toi opened her mouth wide, stuffed it inside, and started sucking it right there in front of me and Rashawn. I have to admit, that shit turned me on.

It must have turned Rashawn on too, because I could feel his penis pulsating through his pants. I looked in his face and saw the thirsty look in his eyes. He wanted his dick sucked too. But he was gonna get much more than that. I had a special treat in store for his fine ass. Toi was my girl, but there was no way I was gonna let this bitch outdo me.

As fast as I could I crawled between his legs. From the way it was poking me, I couldn't wait to get it in my mouth. I undid his belt buckle and hurriedly ripped his pants open. My breath got caught in my throat as I tried to wrap my hand around it.

It was so thick, I couldn't believe it. I couldn't even touch my thumb and my index finger together. Then I tried to stroke it and discovered that it had to be at least ten inches long. For the first time since I was a virgin, I got nervous. I loved a big dick as much as any woman, but this nigga was blessed. My eyes got extra-large when I pulled it out. I was shocked when I wrapped both of my hands around it and the head still showed.

"Dayyyuuumm," I mumbled to myself.

I was an expert at deep throating a dick, but I didn't know how I was gonna get all of that meat into my mouth. I looked over at Toi and the bitch was bobbing up and down on Malcolm's pipe like she was dunking for apples. At that point, Rashawn's dick could have been as long as a baseball bat and I would have tried to stuff it into my mouth. Toi's my girl and all, but there was no way I was going to let her ass outdo me in a fuck contest. Throwing caution to the wind, I quickly lowered my head down onto Rashawn's dick. I stopped abruptly however as the head of his monster hit my tonsils. Knowing that I still had a ways to go before all of it was in my mouth, I tried to relax my throat muscles as much as I could. Slowly and carefully to keep from choking, I eased my head down. With tears welling up in my eyes from his massive sized penis reshaping my mouth, I gagged slightly.

"What's the matter, Candice? Can't take a real dick?" I heard Toi say.

This gave me all the incentive I needed to engulf the rest of it. Once I felt my lips hit his balls, I knew I was there. I had swallowed the whole thing. *Take that bitch,* I would have said if my mouth wasn't filled with dick. Like a certified porn star, I masterfully worked his penis. After slowly easing my moth off of it, I ran my tongue up and down both sides. The more I tasted his chocolate bar the more I got turned on myself. I glanced over at Malcolm and saw that he was cutting his eyes at me. Even though he was receiving his own blow job, courtesy of Toi, he seemed to be very impressed with my skills. After her slick comment, Toi had closed her eyes and went back to sucking Malcolm off, so she didn't notice him sneaking a peak at what I was doing. My pussy was absolutely throbbing. I decided to give Malcolm a show as I increased the speed on the lube job I was giving.

"Oh shit baby, suck that muthafucka," Rashawn screamed.

I didn't think it was possible but I actually felt his dick getting even harder. By now I was feening for it to be inside of me. I glanced over at Malcolm and Toi and saw that he was bending her over and getting ready to enter her from behind. Getting fucked doggy style was the shit, but this night I was in the mood for a different kind of entry.

I reached into my purse, which had fallen on the floor, and pulled out a condom. I then ripped it open with my teeth and proceeded to roll it onto Rashawn's cock. The lust in his eyes was undeniable as he waited for me to mount him. My face held a devilish smile as I climbed aboard his ship. The size of his manhood caused me to ease down on it instead of just jumping on the dick like I usually did.

It completely filled me up as I let my hands rest on his shoulders. Rashawn under-hooked my shoulders and thrust his hips upward, stuffing every inch inside of me. I screamed at the top of my lungs as my body erupted into a mixture of pleasure and pain. Once my pussy loosened up and my juices started flowing, I started riding Rashawn like I was staring in a rodeo. Rashawn cupped my breasts and alternated sucking on both nipples while his dick reshaped my womb. I looked over at Toi. We locked eyes and nodded at each other.

"Damn, bitch, when you gon' cum?" I heard Malcolm ask her. Toi then gave me a look that said, 'not to her ass cum'. I was thinking the same thing. I didn't want to be bothered with her ass bragging on the way back to Kent State that she fucked longer than I did. Both of us held out as long as possible before simultaneously giving way to Mr. Orgasm. By the way his body started to get rigid, I could tell that Rashawn was close to busting his nut as well. He wrapped his arms around my waist and squeezed tightly as he jammed his dick up in me one last time before grunting loudly.

"UUUGHH!"

I could feel his love juice threatening to push through the condom. It had to settle however for its alternate route, which was spilling out of the sides of the Magnum and splashing onto the couch. Exhausted, I laid my head on Rashawn's shoulder. Hesitantly, he wrapped his arms around my shoulders and hugged me. He didn't have to worry.

Shit, I wasn't in love with his ass. I was just tired. After about a minute, I got up off of him and plopped down on the couch. I glanced down at Rashawn's dick, which was still wrapped in the rubber and smiled. He was the best fuck that I'd had in a long time. I knew beyond a shadow of a doubt that my pussy would be sore within twenty-four hours but I didn't give a fuck.

I looked over at Toi and the bitch looked like she was frowning. I don't know why. She'd just gotten dicked down the same way I had. With the noises her ass was making over there, she couldn't tell me that she didn't like it. I scanned the place, trying to remember where the bathroom was.

"Straight down the hall to the right," Malcolm said, reading my mind.

I stood up on wobbly legs and went to relieve myself. A rush of air swirled between my legs and made a sound like wind in a cave. This nigga had really dug me the fuck out! I pee'd for what seemed like thirty minutes. While sitting on the toilet, I groped my tits. This muthafucka had me wanting some more of his dick.

Just thinking about the way pounded me caused my weariness to fade. With renewed energy, I hoped up off the commode and wiped myself. After washing hands, I started back towards the living room. I was ready for some more hot action. As big as Rashwan's dick was, I could only guess that he was used to bitches not being able to withstand his dick game. I wanted to show him that he was dealing with a different type of bitch all together.

As I got closer to the living room, I heard what sounded like arguing. I couldn't hear or understand most of what was being said, but I clearly made out the words 'money', 'fuck' and 'bitch'. I tried to get a little closer so I could be nosey but ended up tripping over a shoe Malcolm had lying in the floor.

I almost fell flat on my face and had to grab the edge of the doorway to keep from falling. When Toi and Rashwan saw me, they immediately painted smiles on their faces. I was about to ask Toi why in the hell she was holding the condom wrapper in her hand when I looked around and saw Malcolm coming through a door on the other side of the room.

"Damn, Candice, you was in there so long, I had to run upstairs and use my other bathroom," he laughed.

When no one else laughed along with him, Malcolm looked around and noticed the strange expressions on everyone's face.

"What the fuck wrong with y'all. Why is everybody looking so strange and shit?" he asked.

That's exactly what the fuck I wanted to know.

12
Candice

    Cathy got up early enough to cook us a good hearty breakfast before we left. I don't know about Toi, but I was extremely grateful. After the night we had, I was hungry as hell. Cathy made it her business to sit next to me.
    When she felt that no one was paying any attention, she slid her hand under the table and up my thigh. I winced slightly as she inserted her middle finger into my vagina. The brutal punishment that Rashawn had inflicted on my womb was starting to surface in a major way. I glanced over at Toi, who was busy devouring a large plate eggs and wondered why she had been so evasive after we'd left Malcolm's crib.
    I asked her about the strange scene in which she and Rashawn were arguing and she just brushed me off, saying that Rashawn owed her some money and that she didn't want Malcolm to find out about it. She also had an answer ready when I asked her why she was holding the condom wrapper in her hand.
    She said that she was just picking it off the floor to throw it away, but for some reason I didn't believe her. The whole thing just seemed weird to me. My pussy was on fire and as much as I loved having something going in and out of it, I had to reach under the table and cut Cathy's finger fucking session short.
    After saying our goodbyes to her parents, Me and Toi hit the highway back to Kent. Now that my fun weekend was over, I had some serious plotting to do. That bitch ass Professor Reynolds was going to pay for going

back on our deal like that. I'd been thinking about it long and hard and I knew just what I was going to do to exact my revenge.

"So, did you enjoy yourself Saturday night?" Toi asked interrupting my thoughts.

"Girl, you know I did. That muthafuckin' Rayshawn is hung like a fuckin' horse! I was struggling to take all that meat!"

"From the looks of things, it looked like he was taking it easy on you. I remember one time he took this bitch in Malcolm's guestroom and destroyed her pussy. When he got finished with her as she was walking sideways," Toi laughed. "He be havin' a hard time gettin' pussy 'cause bitches say his dick is too big. Malcolm told me that he said he would like to see you again, but he don't think you can handle his meat."

"What?" I spat out, insulted. "I can handle anything that muthafucka can put out! I see right now he used to dealing with them shallow pussy hoes! My shit will have that nigga falling in love! Took it easy on me?" I said, mocking her statement. "I didn't pull out all my bag of tricks either."

"That nigga gon' blow yo' muthafuckin spine out," Toi teased, trying to egg me on.

"Shit, bitch you got me fucked up! It ain't a dick hanging low that I can't handle."

Even though I was talking mad shit in front of Toi, I would never talk reckless like that in front of Rashawn. In just that one night, that nigga had earned the fuck outta my respect. Except for a few short conversations about school, that was the extent of our dialog. That was fine by me. After eating such a large breakfast, I was starting to get sleepy. I was even happier when she volunteered to drive all the way.

I couldn't close my eyes fast enough. In less than ten minutes after our conversation stopped, I was in dreamland. When I woke up, Toi was pulling into the parking lot of our dorm. All of a sudden, I got real paranoid wondering if that nigga Byron was going to try some sneak attack type shit. As soon as we got out of the car, I made hurried steps towards the building.

Toi must have been thinking the same thing because she was right on my ass. The elevator seemed like a mile away. This feeling of paranoia had me convinced Byron was going to jump out on our asses. We waited impatiently while we watched the elevator floor numbers drop. The door opened, we both gasped. Standing there live and in color was Byron's silly ass.

"Don't worry," he said, seeing the looks on our faces. "I ain't fuckin' wit' you hoes," he spat as he stared at me. "But you know what? You two bitches are nasty as hell! Y'all need to spray some Lysol in that foul smellin' ass dorm room!"

Byron walked off the elevator laughing while we wondered what the hell he was talking about. As soon as we got off the elevator, we rushed to our dorm room. Looking down at the door, we both noticed that it was cracked open.

"The fuck this nigga done did?" Toi yelled as she pushed the door open. Immediately a foul odor smacked us in the face. As we walked inside, I noticed that the smell seemed to be coming from my side of the room. The closer I got to my bed, the more I felt like gagging.

"Oh no the fuck this nigga didn't!" I screamed. "No the fuck this nasty ass muthafucka didn't piss on my fuckin' bed!"

My comforter was thrown on the floor and piss stains were all over my sheets. I couldn't believe this nigga had the gall to do some fucked up shit like that. All because I didn't want to be bothered with his wack ass no more.

"Candice, look," Toi said pointing to my desk. Anger flowed through me when I saw what his ass had done. You would think that pissing on my bed was enough, but this greasy muthafucka had the nerve to jack off on my fuckin' desk.

"I'm calling the fuckin' police," Toi said pulling out her phone.

"Fuck the cops! Call the muthafuckin' morgue, 'cause I'm kill that muthafucka when I catch up to his ass!"

Ignoring my heated threat, Toi continued dialing. I was too blinded by anger to even hear what she was saying to them. Feeling my temperature reach the boiling point, I grabbed a coffee mug that I'd purchased from one of the local stores and threw it up against the wall.

# # #

Twenty minutes later, the police arrived. The two cops were as different as night and day. One of them, the man, seemed genuinely interested in helping me out. He was ruggedly handsome, with a thick build and soft looking hair. Under normal circumstances, I would have been all over his fine ass. But for right now, all I could think about was having that sick bastard, Byron, thrown in jail. His partner, a husky man looking bitch, looked like she would rather be somewhere eating out some bitch's pussy. I swear this hoe looked like she could be playing football for the Cleveland Browns. She looked at the door and then looked at me and Toi suspiciously.

"There doesn't appear to be any forced entry," she said to us. "Are you girls sure that what you are telling us happened really happened?"

"What the hell is that supposed to mean?" I snapped. "You think we're lying to you or something?"

"Well, this wouldn't be the first time college students called us and said that their place had been broken into and vandalized. Are you sure it wasn't one of your boyfriends that did this? Maybe got a little too loaded and decided to act a fool."

The more she talked, the more livid I became. The nerve of this dyke looking bitch, to come in here and accuse me and my girl of calling them on some bullshit! I tried to calm myself down. I was no fool. I knew that if I continued to be hostile, the chances of them just sweeping this under the rug increased.

"Look. I can positively tell you that it wasn't a boyfriend that did this. Like I said, the asshole's name is Byron Murphy. We dated a few times, I broke it off, and now it seems like his ass can't let go."

"Well, to be honest with you Ms. Robinson, is it?"

I nodded to let the man officer who had spoken know that he was stating my name correctly.

"To be perfectly honest with you, we are not going to be able to arrest him on breaking and entering charges because the door wasn't forced open. Are you sure you didn't give him your key for any reason while you two were dating? If so, he could have made a copy of it. Maybe you left it lying around and he stole it, copied it, and put it back?"

I thought about what the cop was saying to me and if I was honest with myself, I couldn't be sure. I knew I hadn't giving it to his ass, but I guess it was possible that I'd left it lying around and he'd stolen it.

"Plus," he said as if he had more bad news to tell me, "I can pretty much guarantee that he's going to deny doing this, so it will pretty much be your word against his. We can talk to him and see if he slips up and confesses but to be honest…"

The cop held up his palms as if to say we were just shit out of luck.

"In the meantime, I suggest that you have the dorm supervisor change the locks to your door. Do you know if this Byron character still lives at the address you gave us?"

Dejected, I slowly nodded my head.

"Ok, we're gonna run by there and talk to this clown. I'm sorry that we couldn't be more helpful."

As the two cops headed towards the door, I noticed that the female cop was looking at Toi with lust in her eyes. Toi twisted her face up and glared back at her with a disgusted look on her face. The events of this afternoon had changed my plans for the day. Instead of getting started with my plans to get revenge on Professor Reynolds, all I wanted to do drink a little wine and smoke me some calm down.

But first I had to clean up the nasty ass mess that Byron had left for me. At first I wondered why he didn't fuck up Toi's side of the room. Then I remembered that I was the one who was fuckin' this square headed ass nigga. I started pulling the sheets off of my bed and threw them in the clothes basket. I prayed to God that no one was using the washing machine downstairs.

I usually went to the local laundry mat to wash my clothes, but I didn't have time for that this time. I had to get this nigga's pissy smell out of my sheets as soon as possible. After taking the clothes downstairs, I was relieved to see that the washer was unoccupied. As fast as I could, I dumped the sheets into the washer, poured liquid tide on them and started it up. When I got back upstairs, I saw Toi scrubbing my desk down.

"Girl, you didn't have to do that."

"I know I didn't have to do it," Toi said, looking at me as if I'd insulted her. "I did it 'cause you my girl."

"Thanks girl. I appreciate it."

"Hey, you would have done the same for me, right?"

"You know it girl," I said, lying through my teeth. Ain't no way in the fuck I would've cleaned her shit up. Girl or no girl, her ass would have been on her own.

"Alright then, bitch, shut the fuck up and fire that weed up," she said pointing to the blunt lying on her dresser. I couldn't get to it fast enough. I needed a stress reliever in the worse way. After spraying Lysol all over my bed, I plopped down on it and fired up the blunt. A soothing calmness overcame me as I let my problems drift into the air.

"Puff puff pass, bitch. You trying to smoke up all the shit?" Toi asked.

"Oh, my bad."

I passed the blunt to Toi and the two of us proceeded to get gunjafied.

Next Door Nympho 2

13

Candice

For some reason it was hard for me to get out of the bed this morning. I don't know if it was the weed or my body telling me that it needed rest, but I was drowsy as fuck. I looked over at the clock and realized that Professor Reynold's class has already started. It didn't matter though. By the time I got through with his ass, he would be more than happy to give me an A. I got up and dragged myself to the bathroom. After relieving myself, I walked to my desk and turned on my computer. With all the excitement of what had happened when we got back yesterday, I hadn't had a chance to make copies of the little porno movie that I'd made with Professor Reynolds. After logging in to my email account, I saved the video email that Toi had sent me from her phone. Then I downloaded it to a disk. While it was downloading, I took a quick shower. When I got back to the room, Toi was still asleep.

"Hey," I yelled out. "Don't you have class this morning?"

She responded by pulling the covers over her head and going right back to sleep. I shrugged my shoulders, checked the progression of the download, and started getting dressed. When I was done, I brushed my teeth and put my hair in a ponytail. The disc popped out, letting me know that the video had finished downloading. I smiled mischievously as I took the disc out and put it in my purse. I looked over at Toi as I headed for the door and noticed that she was still fast asleep. I started to wake her up but decided against it. I had to hurry if I wanted to get my plan under way. Besides, I ain't no fuckin' alarm clock. I walked out of the building and looked from side to side. The way Byron was acting I didn't know if he would be lurking outside or not. As pissed off as I was though, his ass was in for a surprise if came fuckin' with me today. Although I didn't have my straight razor I was more than ready to swing on his ass. I was slightly disappointed when I didn't see him, but it was all good. I had a plan to execute anyway. I looked at my watch and saw that I had about ten minutes before Professor Reynold's class would be over. Originally, like I'd told Toi I was going to wait before I used this. But the vengeful side of me had me wanting to see this muthafucka squirm as soon as possible. I arrived just as the class was ending. I waited patiently as the students filed out of the classroom. One of the girls asked me why I wasn't in class today.

"Oh, girl I just didn't feel well," I said, clutching my stomach.

Nosey ass bitch. I don't know why hoes can't just mind their own damn business. When the last person walked out, I strutted into the classroom like the boss bitch that I was. My swagger was at an all time high. In just a few short minutes, I was gonna have his ass by the balls. Professor Reynolds was busy shuffling papers when I walked up to his desk.

"May I help you?" he asked without even looking up.

The arrogance of this nigga made me fuckin' sick.
"I don't know," I said. "Can you?"

His head snapped up. A sly smile registered on his face.

"Well, well, well if it isn't Ms. Robinson. Missed you in class this morning," he said sarcastically.

"Is that right?" I responded.

"No, not really. I was just taking a stab at being polite. Now, what can I do for you?" He asked as he leaned back in his chair and interlocked his fingers behind his head.

"You know Richard," I began, calling him by his government name, the name that he'd introduced himself as on the first day of class.

"It's Mr. Robinson to you."

I smirked. Obviously I'd hit a nerve.

"Like I was saying Richard. I'd like to renegotiate the terms of our little agreement."

"Oh really?" He laughed out loud." And just why would I want to do that?"

Without saying a word, I reached into my purse and pulled out the disk. The professor's smile quickly evaporated.

"Why don't you put that into the drive on your lap top and play it. It's a porno movie. I call it 'Confessions of a college Professor'. But I'm thinking about changing the name to something like…Nigga, yo' ass is fucked!"

Professor Reynold's eyes never left me as he inserted the disk into his computer drive. His jaw dropped as he watched me give him some of the best head that he'd ever had in his entire life.

"What the fuck?" he mouthed silently.

"Now, like the fuck I just said. It's time to renegotiate our little agreement!"

Sweat popped onto his forehead as he snatched the disk out of the drive. I reached out my hand to retrieve it and he suddenly snapped it in half.

"Oops," he said, grinning at me.

I looked at him like he was the dumbest fool on earth.

"Muthafucka, how in the fuck did you get to be a Professor?" I asked him. "I know damn well you don't think that's the only copy I have, fool!"

"Dammit," he cursed under his breath. I couldn't believe that he thought I was really that damn stupid.

"I expect my F to be an A by tomorrow or else."

With the elegance of a queen, I turned on my heel and walked away. Just before I went through the door, I turned around. He was staring daggers at me.

"The funny thing is; I was more than willing to let you sample Sprung if you would've just stuck to your word."

The Professor looked at me as if he had no idea who Sprung was.

"Sprung…my pussy, dumb ass! And like I said, I would have been more than willing to give some of it if you wouldn't have acted like a fuckin' slime ball! With that last parting shot, I disappeared through the door and headed to my next class.

14

Unknown

"The fuck you mean, she has a right to know? You ain't said shit to her all this time. Why you wanna run yo' mouth now?"

"I just told you why. She needs to know. It was wrong for me to keep it from her this long. I've had two people that I care about die before having a chance to be truthful with them. I'm not going to make that same mistake with Candice."

This bitch Charmaine was seriously fuckin' up my plans for revenge. After all the talking that I'd done to convince her that it was best that Candice never knew the truth, now she wants to spill the beans. Hell, the only reason I wanted Candice to stay in the dark in the first place was so I could exact my revenge. Now this dumb bitch was threatening to fuck up everything.

"Look, if you tell her now, all it's going to do is confuse the hell out of her and make her hate you for not telling her earlier. She's gonna be pissed off that you kept it from her for so long," I tried to reason with her.

"Whatever happens, happens. But I have an obligation to her."

"To her? The fuck you mean you have an obligation to her? What about your obligation to me?"

"Look. I'm not going to sit here on this phone and argue with you. If you want to tell her, then fine. You can tell her. But I'm only giving you a month to do it. If you haven't done it by then, I'm going to tell her myself."

Click.

"Hello? Hello?"

The phone went dead in my hand. I was so pissed off; I wanted to throw it across the room. My whole body trembled with anger. A month. This bitch was giving me one fuckin' month to get my revenge. Because I sure as hell didn't have any intentions of telling Candice the truth, at least not until I had gotten what I wanted. I got up and paced the floor.

It wasn't that I couldn't execute my plan in the matter of a month. But I wanted to take my time. I wanted to make sure that there wouldn't be any mistakes. I wanted to make sure that this bitch's life was ruined just like the life her mother ruined. And since Charmaine wanted to suddenly develop a conscience, she had just become number 3 on my shit list.

15 *Candice*

After sleeping through half of my math class, I was ready to put the second phase of my plan into motion. I knew arithmetic like the back of my hand so I wasn't worried about failing the class. After all, I was in school to become a math teacher. I'd aced every test or quiz that I'd taken so far, so I wasn't worried about anything in that class. I got to the bus stop just as it was pulling up. As soon as I got on the bus, my cell phone started going off.

"Who the fuck is this calling me so early in the morning?" I complained. A few of the older patrons on the bus looked at me like I was being disrespectful but I didn't give a fuck. I'm a grown ass woman and if I want to cuss, then I'm going to fuckin' cuss. I looked at my cell and saw that it was Toi. I guess her lazy ass decided to get up out of the bed after all.

"What's up girl?" I answered.

"Girl, I feel sick as fuck. I think my mother poisoned my ass."

"Stop trippin'. I ate the same thing you did, and I feel fine. I see you finally decided to get up, huh?"

"Hell nah. I'm still in the fuckin' bed. And I'ma stay in this muthafucka until I feel better. I heard you leave out earlier. You went to Professor Reynold's class? After the shit he tried to pull? I don't know if I coulda done that. I woulda been up there tryin' to scratch that nigaa's eyes out."

"Relax, homegirl," I said laughing. "I got that situation all taken care of."

"Oh yeah?" She said, sounding as if she perked up a bit. "Girl what the fuck did you do? You gotta give me the details of that shit."

"I'll tell you when I get back to the dorm room. I can't talk about it right now."

"Girl I can't wait to hear what you did to that muthafucka."

"Well, I ain't done with his ass yet. Now it's on to phase two. I gotta go," I told her, seeing that the bus was about to come to my stop. Beady little eyes stared at me as I exited the bus.

"I'm glad she's getting off," I heard one of the older women say.

"Fuck you old hoes," I shot back. It may have been disrespectful, but the way I see it is you have to give respect to get it and but making that comment, her ass was disrespecting me. The driver looked at me like I was totally out of line. Well, fuck him too. As I stepped off the bus, I peered at my destination and smiled. I walked through the parking lot of Walmart and made my way inside. I was on a mission. It was time to exercise my womanly charms.

"Excuse me, but do yo know if Jason still works here?" I asked one of the greeters. Of course I knew that he did.

"Yeah. He works in the music department," the short, fat lady told me. "It's back there," she said pointing towards the right.

"Ok. Thank you."

"Don't mention it."

As I walked away, I felt strange. I glanced back to see the greeter staring at me. No doubt she was jealous of me because my body was banging and she looked all dumpy and shit. Bitches kill me with that shit. Don't be mad at me cause your shit ain't tight. Get your ass in the gym.

Because I didn't know what Jason looked like, I had to browse the music area until I found out who he was. When I was fuckin' around with Byron, he'd told me that Professor Reynolds had a son that worked there. Since he'd taken the Professor's class previously, I figured he knew what hell he was talking about.

I guess the muthafucka was good for something. After looking through the rap section for a few minutes, I heard someone say, "Jason, what time do you get off?" I turned around to see a young man with thick glasses checking his watch. This clown was the definition of a nerd.

"In about ten minutes," he said.

"Shit," I mumbled to myself, figuring that I was going to have to work fast in order to get started on my plan. But then I saw the young lady who'd asked him what time he got off walk up to him.

"Don't you want to do me a favor?" She asked. "Don't you want to stay here for another hour and let me go home instead? It's more money for you."

"But I got stuff to do Tracy."

"Oh, come on, baby, please?"

The girl started rubbing his arm. I paid close attention to see how he would react to a females touch. This nigga stated giggling like a little kid. I swear if he had a tail he would have wagged it. I just shook my head. If this little hot in the ass teenager could make this nigga turn to putty, he didn't stand a chance against a bitch like me.

"Yeah, ok," Jason said, smiling from ear to ear.

"Thanks, hon."

The girl then scampered off, presumably to tell her boss that Jason was going to work the remainder of her shift. Seconds later, an older white guy came out and looked at Jason like he was crazy.

"Jason, did you agree to work the rest of Tracy's shift?"

"Uh, yeah. Is that ok?"

The older man ran his hand over his face. It took everything in me not to start laughing. It was obvious that the girl had taken advantage of him before.

"Jason, why do you keep letting Tracy and the other girls that work here do that to you? I can pretty much promise you that if you asked them to work for you, they would say no."

"Nah, I doubt it, Mr. White. Matter of fact, I think Tracy likes me."

Mr. White just shook his head and walked away. I applauded him for trying to help the disillusioned young man out, but he didn't have to worry. By the time I got through with his ass, he wouldn't know Tracy or any other young bitch that worked there was alive. As soon as Mr. White was gone, I made my move.

"Excuse me, but could you help me find a CD please."

Jason looked over at me and his eyes lit up like neon lights. He stared at me for a few seconds. The unmistakable look of lust in his eyes told me that this game was over before it even started. At first I thought it would take a couple of weeks for the plan to work. Now I see it will only take a few days. Once I slapped Sprung on his ass and gave him a super blowjob, it would be a wrap.

"Hellooo," I said, getting tired of him staring at me like I was on display.

"Oh, I'm sorry. Yes, of course I can help you," he said, trying to sound professional and cool at the same time.

Jason walked around the end cap and clumsily bumped into it while he was still staring at me. I didn't want to embarrass him anymore than he already was, so I pretended that I didn't see it. When he got halfway to me, I pulled out my dorm room keys and dropped them on the floor. Then I bent over and picked them up. I didn't have to look back to know that he was probably drooling over the sight of my fat ass. I shook it slightly from side to side, just to make sure that he knew what I was working with. He tried to act like he wasn't looking when I stood up and turned around, but I knew better than that.

"How can I help you?" he asked smiling.

"I was looking for the Rhianna CD. I don't know the name of it, though."

Jason looked up in the air, trying to think of the CD he thought I would be referring to. All of a sudden he snapped his fingers.

"Oh, you're probably talking about *Unapologetic*."

"Yeah, I think so," I said, going with the flow. "Is that her newest one?"

"Yeah, that's her latest release. But it's not in the rap section. It's in the R&B section."

"Oh. Now I feel stupid."

"Nah, you don't have to feel stupid. It's my job to help you find what you need. Follow me."

Jason walked a few feet down from where we were and picked out the CD. I could tell that he was trying to look cool to impress me but he was doing a piss poor job of it. He just seemed awkward.

"Here you go pretty lady," he said handing it to me.

I gave him a fake smile and batted my eyes.

"You think I'm pretty?"

"Hell yeah," he responded. "I think you're beautiful."

I stared into his eyes for a few seconds, trying to get him to believe that I was actually feeling his corny ass.

"Well, I wasn't going to say anything because I didn't want to play myself, but I think you are one of the most handsome men that I have seen in a long time."

Jason put his head down and started blushing. This was going to be like taking candy from a fuckin' baby.

"Hey, what time do you get off?" I asked as if I didn't already know. "I'm kind of hungry and I was thinking that maybe we could go and get something to eat."

"For real?"

"Yeah. I'm fuckin' starvin'. Let's roll out."

A wide smile appeared across Jason's face. But then, just as quickly as it came it went away.

"Oh shit," he said in a disappointed tone. "I don't get off for another hour."

"Oh. Oh well. I guess it wasn't meant to be, then."

I turned and walked to the counter to pay for my purchase. Just like I thought he would be, Jason was right on my ass.

"Wait. I mean, can't you just come back up here when I get off? I got paid today and I would love to treat you to lunch."

"I don't know," I said, playing hard to get. I believe in signs and this might be one of them. Maybe we weren't meant to be bothered with each other."

"Well, we could take it as a sign that I worked past my scheduled shift. If it wasn't for that we would have never met each other. Someone else would have been helping you instead of me."

"I guess that is true. I'll tell you what. I have a few things to take care of, but if I can, I'll stop back up here and you can take me to lunch."

"Cool! That's what's up," he said excitedly. After paying for my CD I hurried home so I could get ready to put a spell on Jason.

# # #

When I got back to the dorm room, I discovered that Toi wasn't there, which was a relief in itself. I didn't feel like hearing the fifty questions that her ass would have hit me with. I would explain it all to her in due time.

After showering, I threw on the tightest pair of jeans I had and blouse that was way more revealing than it should have been. The baby oil I applied to my skin had it glistening like new money. The perfume I doused on myself had me horny so I knew what it would do for Jason.

Just as I got ready to run out the door, my cell phone rang. Seeing that it was my aunt, I started not to answer it. But since she was supporting me financially, I guess the least I could do was talk to her. My aunt sent me one thousand dollars a month and I was grateful but sometimes I just didn't want to be bothered with her sadness. I know she feels bad for me because of what happened to my mother and my grandmother, but she acts like it's her fault.

"Hello?" I answered.

"Hey Candice! What is my favorite niece up to?"

"Favorite niece? Aunt Charmaine, I'm your only niece," I reminded her laughing.

"Yeah I know. Listen, I didn't really want anything. I just wanted to tell you that I dropped your check in the mail today."

"Oh, ok. Aunt Charmaine, I really appreciate you sending me money like this."

"I'm glad to do it. But look. I'm coming up there in the next few weeks or so. You sound like you're in a hurry so I'm gonna let you go, but there is something I want to talk to you about."

"Oh yeah? What is it?" I asked.

"It can wait until then. Besides. I want to tell you in person anyway. Take care girl. I love you."

"I love you too, Aunt Charmaine."

I guess whatever she wanted to talk to me about was not that important, since she said it could wait. Oh well. I had bigger fish to fry anyway.

16

Candice

I got back to Wal-Mart about thirty minutes later than I said I would and just like I figured, 'ol soft ass Jason was standing in front of the store looking around. There was no doubt in my mind that he was searching for me. I stood behind a tree, peeking out from behind it. I was enjoying the sad look on his face when he thought that I'd stood him up. I know its sadistic but, hey…what the fuck ever. When I got tired of him looking like a lost puppy, I strolled across the parking lot. I was about to call his name when he spotted me. The nigga smiled so hard I could count all thirty two of his teeth, even from the long distance I was at. Jason breathed a huge sigh of relief when I walked up to him.

"Damn, girl. I was starting to think you wasn't gonna show up," he said, still smiling.

"I told you if I could, I would. I'm a woman of my word baby. So, where are we going to eat?"

"You're choice. Where do you want to go?"

"We can go to Applebee's. I love the chicken fingers."

"Cool. My ride's over there," he said pointing to a Blue Toyota Corolla.

As we walked towards his car, I grabbed his hand. Then I glanced down at his crotch and just as I suspected, this muthafucka had a full scale hard on. It was as obvious as me being a dime piece that this nigga wasn't used to bitches giving him attention.

"Wait," I said just before we got to his car. "How old are you?" I asked as if it mattered.

"Huh?" He asked confused. Apparently the question had caught him off guard.

"I asked you how old you were. Because I'm twenty years old and the last thing I want is to be going to jail for fuckin' with a minor."

"Oh," he said, laughing. "I'm nineteen, baby so we straight."

I studied him intently to see if detected a lie in his answer. When I was satisfied that he was telling me the truth, I resumed walking. It didn't really matter to me how old he was, but the effect would be much more devastating if he were legal. Being the perfect gentleman, Jason opened the car door for me and closed it once I got inside. Once he got inside, he unclipped his cell phone and made a call.

"Hey mom. I was just calling to tell you that I wasn't going to be able to pick up your dry cleaning for another hour. Something came up."

I smiled wickedly. This nigga hadn't known me a good hour and already he was putting me ahead of his family.

"It really makes me feel special that you're willing to postpone whatever you have to do with your mom and take me to lunch," I told him in the most humble voice I could muster up.

"It's cool. I just have to pick up her shit from the cleaners."

"Still," I said running my hand up and down his thigh. "No one ever treated me this special before." I was pouring it on thick. As if by accident, I let my hand fall into his lap and brush up against his meat.

"Sorry about that," I said, quickly removing my hand.

Putting my head down as if I were embarrassed, I cut my eyes towards him and saw a broad smile erupt on his face. Once we got to the restaurant, he hopped out and ran around to the passenger's side. He was all too happy to open the door for me.

"After you, pretty lady," he said ushering me to the front of the eatery. The place was more crowded than I expected it to be this time of the day. Even still, we didn't have to wait that long to be seated. When the waitress beckoned for us to follow her, she led us to a booth in the far corner of the restaurant. We sat down and I quickly scanned the room, trying to see if I recognized anyone. I didn't. The one thing that did catch my eye though was the two cops who were sitting at a table about twenty-five feet from us. I couldn't see their faces but I was wondering if they were the same policemen who answered me and Toi's call.

"You know what you want, besides the chicken fingers?" Jason asked.

"Nah, I'm gonna have to look at the menu a little more. That's a nice phone," I said to him, eyeing his I Phone 4 S.

"Thanks. My dad got it for me for my birthday."

"Can I see it," I asked him.

Jason hesitated for a second.

"Boy, I ain't gonna take your phone. I was just thinking about upgrading and it crossed my mind to get one of these."

"Oh, ok," he said, sliding his phone to me.

"Wow, you don't trust me already," I said. "That has to be a sign."

"Huh? Oh no, yes I do."

"Really? 'Cause you didn't act like it just then."

"Nah, I ain't tripping over no phone," he said before picking up the menu and scanning it. This was my chance to do what I had to do. All of a sudden I started sneezing violently.

"Oh God, excuse me," I said as I jumped up and headed for the bathroom.

Before Jason could say anything I was gone, still clutching his cell phone in my palm. As soon as I got in the bathroom, I went straight for the contacts. I knew exactly how to access it, since I had the same exact phone. All I needed was one number. As fast as I could, I pulled up the number for dad. I then reached inside my purse, took out a pen, and copied the number down. After stuffing the numbers in my purse, I calmly walked back out of the bathroom and headed back for our table. But on the way there, I made sure to walk past the cops to see if they were the ones who came to our dorm room. They weren't.

"Sorry about that," I said once I got back to the table. "These damn allergies act up at the damndest times. Did you figure out what you want to eat yet?" I asked him, slyly sliding his phone back across the table to him.

"Yeah. I think I gonna get this Chicken Portabella," he said, pointing at the menu.

"Ok, I'll just get an order of fries to go along with my Chicken Fingers."

After the waitress came and took our orders and left, I was about to do some more mind fucking on my young target when all of a sudden I heard loud laughter coming from the table to our far right. My blood boiled as I looked over and saw Byron and a couple of other players from the football team giggling like some hoes. Jason must have noticed the change in my demeanor. He looked at them and looked back at me.

"You know them dudes?" he asked.

"I know one of them," I told him figuring that I had no reason to lie about it. "I used to date that square headed nigga in the blue Polo shirt."

Again, Byron and his crew broke out into laughter as they looked over at me. I could only imagine what he was saying. I wondered if he'd told them that he was trying to beg me to get back together with his ass? Or that he had to result to vandalism because I would no longer give his ass the time of day?

"Maybe I should go over there and holla at that nigga," Jason said, half-heartedly. It was obvious that he only said that to gain my favor. I was half tempted to let him go over there, but knowing that Byron and his friends would have beaten the breaks off his young ass caused me to grab his arm.

"Nah, don't worry about it Jason. That nigga just jealous because I'm with you and not with his tired ass."

Jason eased back down in the chair. I looked over to their table and saw that Byron was staring directly at me. *'Oh this nigga wanna play games huh,'* I thought to myself. *'Ok, I'ma show his ass how to play games.'* As smooth as water, I got up from my side of the booth and went over to Jason's side.

"You know, you're one sexy ass dude," I whispered into his ear. At the same time I was grabbing is dick, I was sticking my tongue in his ear. I could almost feel Byron's eyes burning a hole through the back of my head as I turned Jason's face around and started tonguing him down. I kissed him for a good fifteen seconds before I heard someone clearing their throat. I looked up to see the waitress holding our food and grinning.

"Oh, I'm sorry," I said sliding back over to my side of the booth. "We got carried away for a minute there."

"Yeah, I saw," she said, still smiling. I glanced over at Byron and noticed that he wasn't grinning anymore. I could tell that his boys were him giving grief about his ex being all up on another muthafucka right in front of him. *'Take that, bitch ass nigga.'* Byron tried to force a smile on his face as if it wasn't bothering him, but I knew better.

He looked like he wanted to come over and start some bullshit, but I guess the two big ass cops sitting there changed his mind. After waving his hand towards our table, Byron and his boys got up to leave. I guess he had already paid for the meal since no one tried to stop him. Byron made it a point to walk pass our booth on his way out the door.

"Candice. How you doing sweetheart? I didn't see you over here."

"Is that right?" I said, playing right along with his little game.

"Oh, I gotta go," he said looking at his watch as if he were suddenly in a hurry. Then he leaned down and whispered in my ear. "Hey, how's your roommate doing?"

17

Charmaine

Sitting on my couch, I stared at the picture of my mother. She's wearing brown t-shirt with writing on it that says *Family Over All*. That was her mantra. She firmly believed that whatever problems a family had within it, they could always be worked out.

"I'm sorry mama," I said as I got up and walked over to the mantle.

Picking it up, I wipe dust off of it as tears formed in the corners of my eyes. Maybe I'd made a mistake revealing that I was going to tell Candice the truth about everything. Or at least I shouldn't have told the person I told. But I don't care what anybody says, Candice deserves to know the full story. I know that I'm taking a big chance by telling them what the real deal is.

But she is my niece. I already feel bad that I've kept it from her this long. Maybe the asshole is right. Maybe she will hate me for not telling her about it sooner. But that's just a chance that I am going to have to take. I have to believe that in time she will find it in her heart to forgive me. She's all I have and I just couldn't bear to think she would hate me forever.

The same blood that flows through my veins flows through hers. She has to realize that. After sitting the picture down, I walked slowly into the kitchen, grabbed a glass out of the cabinet and poured me a shot of Ciroc. I know it's early but I don't give a damn about that anymore. Hell, why should I? It's not like I can undo what has already been done. But what I can do is right a wrong that has been going on for several years. And in the matter of a few weeks, that's just what I planned on doing.

18

<u>Candice</u>

I had Jason drop me off at the corner down the street from my dorm room. I had no desire for him to know where I lived. Once he got a taste of Sprung, he wasn't going to like it when I took it away from him. He was just a means to an end. I had no intentions of falling in love with him or making him my boyfriend.

I just wanted to get back at his punk ass father. As soon as he let me out, I power walked up the sidewalk. The way Byron had whispered into my ear about Toi sent a chill through my spine. I had to get home and check on her. I'd tried to call her, but she wasn't answering her cell phone. After running inside the dorm building, I punched the elevator button and waited. In my mind, it was taking too long so I abandoned that idea and ran up the stairs.

When I got to the door, it was once again slightly ajar. But instead of easing inside, this time I pushed it open with force and ran in. My heart dropped as I saw Toi tied up to a chair. Her wrists were duck taped behind her and her body was duck taped to the chair.

There was a sock stuffed in her mouth and more duct tape covering her mouth wrapped around her head. As fast as I could, I ran over to her and started tearing the tape loose. Upon having the tape removed from her mouth, Toi tried to gather as much air into her lungs as possible.

"You ok?" I asked, frantically trying to free my friend.

Still not able to speak yet, Toi nodded her head.

"I'm calling the fuckin' police," I said, snatching out my cell phone. I got as far as three numbers before Toi reached up and grabbed my arm.

"It's not gonna do any good, girl," she said, regaining her voice.

"The fuck you mean it's not going to do any good? Wasn't it Byron that did this sick ass shit to you?" It wasn't until just then that I noticed the bruise on the left side of Toi's cheek.

"And that muthafucka hit you too? Ah hell nah, his ass gotta go to jail for real now!"

"Candice wait. It's not gonna do any good to call the police."

"Why the fuck not? It was Byron that did this shit, wasn't it?"

"I think so, but I can't be sure."

"Ok, you're going to have to explain to me what the fuck you're talkin' about, 'cause your're confusing the fuck out of me!"

"Damn, bitch, if you'd just calm down for a second I'll tell you. I couldn't identify the nigga 'cause he had on a mask. I mean it sounded like him, but that shit won't hold up on court."

I was stunned. This muthafucka was getting on my last nerve with this shit. Not only had he broken into our home, pissed on my bed, and jacked off on my desk. Now he was assaulting my roommate and friend.

"So that's what the fuck he meant by that comment at Applebee's," I mumbled to myself.

"Comment? What comment?" Toi asked. "And when did yo see that muthafucka at Applebee's?"

"You know what? Let's just get you cleaned up first. I'll tell you about it at the bar."

"The bar?"

"Yeah, girl the bar. I need a fuckin' drink."

Toi walked to her dresser and took out an already rolled blunt.

"Here. Fire that up while I get cleaned up. After the morning I had, I need more than a fuckin' drink."

"You ain't fuckin' lying," Toi aid. "And don't worry. We'll get that muthafucka back one way or another."

# # #

The kush was just what we needed to calm our nerves. I don't know where the hell she got that shit from but it sure as hell did the trick. Even though the earlier events had us fucked up, we decided that we were going to kick back and relax for the night. The bar we went to had live music, cute men, and strong drinks. That was a recipe to get out groove, freak, and lush on.

"Don't you wanna pat us down," Toi asked the muscle bound security guard.

"Girl get on away from me before you start something you can't finish," he answered. He was looking at both of us like he wanted to eat us up.

"Baby, I guarantee you, anything that I start I can damn well finish," Toi replied sassily.

"Girl bring yo' ass on," I told her as we walked in and started looking for somewhere to sit down.

Toi had done a pretty good job with the bruise on her face. The make-up she'd put on pretty much hid the mark. There were a few seats at the bar, so we quickly made our way to them before someone else beat us there. As soon as we sat down, the men were all over us. I could see why too. Looking around, all I could see was a bunch of homely looking ass broads.

"Now I know you two ladies are gonna give me the pleasure of buying y'all some drinks," a tall skinny brother with deep brush waves asked us. Although he wasn't that cute, when I looked down at his package to see what he was working with, I was more than pleased.

It wasn't as large as Rashawn's monster, but it was in no way disappointing. Right away I started visualizing it poking around in one of my holes. Before either one of us could answer his question, another fool walked trying to get his mack on.

"Damn, you two ladies sho' look good tonight," he said licking his lips. The way he was licking his lips reminded me of LL Cool J. Me and Toi looked at each other and right away knew that we were thinking the same thing. Not only were we going to get our chill and drink on tonight. But chances were starting to look good that we were both gonna end up with our legs in the air.

"Well, thanks for the compliment," I said, "but if y'all really wanna do us a favor, you could start off by buying me and my girl a drink."

The two of them looked at each other. One of them dug into his pocket, while the other one pulled out his wallet.

"I got it, homie," the skinny brother said.

"Nah, save ya bread, my dude. I got everybody. You can get the next round," the lip licker said.

Shrugging his shoulders, the tall guy stuffed his money back in his pocket, while the other one called out to the barmaid. Me and Toi ordered Cosmopolitans while the fellas got a shot of Hennessey and a shot of Vodka, respectively.

"What's ya name, handsome?" I asked the one paying for the first round.

"My name's Mark, baby, and you are?" He said, extending his hand.

"I'm Candice," I replied.

"And what's yo' name, sweet thing," the other guy asked Toi.

"Toi. And you are…"

"Dex, baby."

Toi looked him up and down and shrugged her shoulders. Dex made a face as if the gesture offended him, but didn't say anything. When the drinks arrived, Toi finished hers off in less than two minutes.

"Damn girl, you taking it to the head ain't you?"

"Whateva girl," she said waving me off. "I'm here to let loose tonight."

Out of the corner of my eye, I saw Dex grinning devilishly. I knew exactly what that nigga was thinking. I hoped that Mark was thinking the same thing 'cause I was more than ready to get dicked down tonight.

"Fuck it," I said raising the glass up to my lips. "Bottoms up."

Since it took this bitch two gulp to get done with her drink, I had to do mine in one. Friend or no friend, I wasn't about to be upstaged by her ass. As the last drop of liquor went down my throat, I ran my tongue around the rim of the glass.

"Damn, baby it's like that?" Mark asked.

"You damn skippy it is," I replied lustfully.

When I saw Toi rolling her eyes in a jealous manner, I knew that my point had been made. The conversation between the four of us was just getting hot and heavy when my cell phone vibrated. After checking the screen and seeing that it was Jason, I sent it directly to voice mail. I'll deal with his nerdy ass later. Tonight was dick hunting night.

"Boyfriend checkin' up on you?" Mark asked.

"Nigga please. I ain't attached to no muthafucka," I stated proudly.

"I hear that pretty lady. So I ain't gotta worry about no nigga rollin' up on me and tryin' to put the hurt on me?"

"Nah, baby. The only thing you have to worry about putting the hurt on you is this pussy."

"Is that right?" He asked with a gleam in his eye.

Before I could answer him, my cell phone vibrated again. Trying to suppress a smile as I looked at the screen, I lied and told Mark that it was my mother and that I had to take the call. When I got inside the bathroom, I ducked into the last stall for a little privacy.

"Hello," I answered sexily while closing the door.

"Hey beautiful. I was just calling to touch base with you and to see if you enjoyed yourself while you were in C-Town," Rashawn said.

"I sure did baby," I said, remembering how Rashawn pumped his love bone in and out of me.

"Matter of fact, I was hoping that we could get together again the next time you were in town."

"Oh most definitely," I said, trying to contain my excitement.

"Cool. So when so you think that will be?" He asked.

Damn this nigga sounded sexy as hell!

"I don't know just yet. I'ma have to check with Toi and find out when she's visiting her parents again. She's the one with the car, so I have to wait on her."

"Oh, ok. But if she takes too long, I'm just gonna have to hit the highway and pay you a visit, sweet thang."

My pussy did somersaults at the mention of him coming to see me.

"Oh yeah, I'm definitely down for that," I said excitedly.

"Look, I'm not gonna hold you all night. I just wanted to make sure that we kept in touch. I'll call you back in a day or so."

"Ok. Talk to you later." After hanging up from Rashawn, I opened the door to the stall and was startled to see Toi staring me in the face.

"The fuck wrong with you?" I asked her.

"Nothin'. Just wondering how long you were gonna be in here trying to make a long distance love connection."

"Mind ya business, bitch," I said brushing past her.

"Oh, so now you wanna treat a bitch like that, huh?" She said laughing. "As I recall, I'm the one who introduced you to Rashawn, so don't get funky."

"You right girl, you right," I said realizing that I was trippin'.

At first, I wondered how she knew who I was talking to. I hadn't told her that me and Rashawn had exchanged numbers. But just as quickly, it came to my mind that the bitch was probably eavesdropping at the bathroom stall door. As I was about to walk out of the bathroom, Toi grabbed my arm.

"Hold up a sec," she said digging into her purse. "Here."

"Why are you giving me your car keys?"

"I don't need them. I'm going back to Dex's place. You can take Mark to the dorm room."

"Back to his place?" I asked her as if I hadn't heard her right. "Toi, are you sure that's safe?" I asked with genuine concern. I may be selfish but the last thing I want is for something to happen to my roommate.

"Girl, that nigga harmless," she said waving her hand towards the door. "Besides, after I put this good loving on his ass, he ain't gonna be able to do much of nothing."

We both laughed at the comment.

"Now let's get out there before somebody steals our men for the night."

"Oh please," I said. "These homely looking ass hoes ain't got nothing on a bitch like me."

I noticed that the bar had gotten a lot more crowded since I was in the bathroom. I looked over to the spot where we were sitting and noticed some fat cock-eyed bitch all up in Mark's face. Normally I woulda just said fuck it and moved on to the next nigga, but since I was so hot and Mark had a rather impressive package hanging below his waist, I decided to get rid of this bitch. Since Toi had decided to drape herself in jewelry before we left the dorm, I figured that I would use it to my advantage. Our hands and fingers were pretty much the same size which would come in handy for what I was about to do.

"Toi, let me borrow your ring right quick. "

"Girl, what you about to do?" She asked. I had a sinister look on my face so I knew she could tell that I as up to no good.

"You'll see. This is how you get rid of a hoe without getting violent with the bitch." Toi smirked as she twisted the ring off of her finger.

"Teach me, oh great one," she said sarcastically.

Taking the ring from her, I slid it onto my left ring finger. I then stomped over to where Mark and Dex were standing and went into my act.

"Nigga no the fuck you didn't bring your ass to the bar and trick off on some bitch and you got three little ones at home!"

I was just loud enough for Mark, Dex, Toi, and the cock eyed bitch to hear, but not too loud as so everyone else could hear.

"Uh…who the fuck is she?" The woman asked Mark. Before he could say a word, I spoke up for him.

"Who am I? Who the fuck am I? Bitch, who the fuck are you? But to answer yo' question, I'm the bitch who's got papers on his ass," I yelled, holding up my left hand. The woman looked at Mark, who was now staring at me with his mouth open.

"I thought you told me that you was single."

"Well, bitch the nigga lied to yo' ass!"

The woman looked at me with a scowl on her face.

"You know what? You got one more time to call me a bitch and I'ma…"

"You gon' do what, bitch?" I asked her, sticking my hand in my purse. Toi followed my lead, sliding her hand in her purse as well. Seeing that she was in a no-win situation, the woman wisely backed down. My straight razor was back in Cleveland at Toi's parent's house and I doubted if she had anything on her but the woman didn't know that.

"Look, the nigga told me that he was single girl," the woman said raising her hands in surrender. "I ain't trying to get involved in no drama or bullshit. Ain't no nigga worth that."

The woman walked away without saying another word.

"What the fuck just happened here?" Mark asked, looking at Dex. Dex simply shrugged his shoulders. He was just as confused as Mark was.

"That's called getting rid of a bum bitch," I spat. "And now that Nell Carter is out of the fuckin' way, let's get the fuck outta here Mark so you can see what it's like to get some pussy from a top shelf, grade A bitch. See you in the morning home girl," I told Toi just before grabbing Mark's hand and pulling him towards the door.

19

Candice

As soon as we got in the car, Mark started up on some 'let's get to know each other bullshit.' Fuck that! I didn't want to get to know his ass that way. I didn't want to know his middle name, where he worked at, or none of that bullshit. All I wanted him to do was stick his dick up in me as far as it would go and pump as hard as he could. To make sure that this nigga knew exactly what his purpose was, I reached over and clutched his dick before we'd even made it out of the parking lot.

"Oh shit," he moaned when I gave it a gentle squeeze. Mark was rock hard and I knew why. Of course I was a fine bitch, but that was only part of the reason. If his ass would have been paying attention to what I was doing at the bar instead of focusing n my ass and tits, he would have seen me sprinkle a crushed up Viagra pill into his drink.

I know. Usually it's a man that pulls some foul shit like that. But as hot and horny as I was, I wasn't taking any chances tonight. I needed a hard Nestle crunch bar not a marshmallow dick. Eagerly, I unzipped his pants and reached inside. It felt like a steel rod as I tried to pull it out.

It was so hard, I had to unbuckle his belt and loosen his pants all the way in order to get it all the way free. It was gorgeous. Not as big as Rashawn's but it would more than serve its purpose. My mouth seemed to have a mind of its own as my lips parted. My tongue followed suit as it dipped down and danced on the top of the head. He almost lost control of the vehicle when I engulfed his entire manhood. I stopped immediately, knowing that Toi would go ballistic if this nigga wrecked her shit. She'd be pissed off if she even knew I'd let him drive her whip.

"Shit girl, why you stop?"

"'Cause I don't want to die, nigga that's why. We'll continue this shit when we got to my dorm room."

The disappointment on Mark's face was evident. But fuck that. I cared about my life way more than I care about his damn feelings. I cut my eyes at him as he pulled into the parking lot. It suddenly dawned on me that he knew where my dorm was, although I hadn't given him any directions.

"Have you been here before?" I asked.

"Huh? Oh, nah, I haven't," he stuttered.

I had never seen him around, so he may have been telling the truth. But my gut instinct told me that his ass was lying. It didn't matter though. Even if he was boning some other bitch in the dorm, which I suspected was the case, he was my meat for tonight.

After he parked the car and got out, I led him to my building. I thought I was walking fast, but this nigga was practically running at a chance to get the pussy. Impatiently, he tapped his foot as we waited for the elevator doors to open. They couldn't open fast enough as we slid inside the elevator and quickly attacked each other.

Our tongues aggressively explored each other's mouths as we kissed each other passionately. Marks strong hands found their way to my ass and groped it with vigor. Pausing for a second to push the button to my floor did nothing to slow down the sexual momentum.

"How does that feel baby?" I asked him as I grabbed his hand and guided it under my skirt. A wry smile spread across his face when he discovered that I didn't have any panties on.

"Mhmmm," I moaned as his middle finger entered my love cave. Pussy juice ran down his arm and dripped off the end of his elbow as he finger fucked me.

"Got Damn, I can't wait to get up in this shit," he claimed.

The elevator doors were half open when we ran out of it and sprinted to my room. After opening the door, we couldn't tear each other's off fast enough. My pussy was hotter than Mexican chilli.

Buttons popped off my blouse, hit the floor, and scattered under the bed as I'd gotten tired of fumbling with it so I just ripped it off. Mark then reached behind my back and unhooked my bra clasp, causing my titties to spring forward like a cheetah on its prey.

Mark then pushed me down on the bed and grabbed my legs just above my calves. With light force he pushed them up towards my head. I cried out in ecstasy as Mark drove his face into my patch. Sprung dripped all over his chin as he devoured me.

"Oh hell yeah, baby, eat that pussy! Eat that pussy, just like that," I begged.

Mark proceeded to eat my coochie like it was icing on a cake. It felt so good to me; I decided to give him a helping hand. Reaching down with both fingers, I gently touched my pussy lips and pulled them apart wider.

Mark lapped at my clit for a few seconds longer before he started tongue fucking me. I grabbed the back of his head and pushed, trying to force Mark to the last section of my womb. He hesitated for a second, which partially set me off.

"Muthafucka, you'd better not! You better not stop eating that pussy," I screamed.

"I won't baby," he mumbled as he started licking again.

Twenty seconds later, a sea of my lust liquid gushed out and saturated his chin. When Mark told me to turn over on my stomach, I thought I was getting ready to get the meat, but he had other ideas. Grabbing my hips gently, Mark lifted my ass in the air.

"Oh shit," I yelled out, gripping the sheets as Mark did the unthinkable.

After spreading my ass cheeks, Mark began to lick my asshole in a slow rhythmic motion. The sensational feeling of Mark tossing my salad drove me wild. Cum poured out of me like a faucet.

"Oh My God!!" I screamed out.

With the sexual appetizers out of the way, it was now time for the main course. Mark must have been reading my mind as he turned me back over. After retrieving a condom from his pants pocket, he rolled it on and prepared to enter me.

"Ooooo yeeessss," I purred when he stuck it in. Wanting to feel it all, I wrapped my legs around his back and used them to try and pull every inch of him inside of me. I closed my eyes and drifted to bliss.

"Yeah, you like this shit, don't you bitch? You like the way I'm hitting this pussy, don't you?"

"Oh, hell yeah, baby beat that pussy up!"

For some strange reason it was turning me on to hear him call me out of my name while he was fucking me. I was definitely on the verge of busting another nut. Before I could, however, he unwrapped his legs from around his back and put them on his shoulders. From then on, Mark proceeded to fuck the lining out of my pussy. And I was enjoying every delicious stroke!

Because I was loving the feeling so much, I tried to hold off on having my third orgasm but I just couldn't. A split second after I came all over the rubber, Mark filled up the inside of it. I bellowed so many nasty and dirty things out of my mouth that even know what I was saying.

"Oh shit," Mark said, collapsing onto the bed next to me.

I was worn the fuck out but satisfied as hell. After catching my breath, my mind traveled back to the figure I thought I'd seen running out of my room. I turned to Mark and was about to mention it to him until I noticed him looking at me strangely.

"The fuck you looking at me like that for? I know you ain't about to tell me that my shit ain't the bomb."

"Nah baby, it ain't that. Matter if fact, you got some of the best pussy I ever had in my life."

"What then?" I asked.

"I thought you said that you was single."

"I am single," I said confused.

"Then who the fuck is Rashwan?"

Next Door Nympho 2

20

Candice

Sleep didn't come easy for me as I tossed and turned all night. With the way Mark put the dick on me, I shoulda slept the night away. Sometime during the night, Toi crept her ass in and was snoring rather loudly when my alarm went off, indicating that it was time for me to get up and get ready for class.

As soon as the noise hit my ears, I knew that I wasn't going to my first class. Then I decided that I wasn't going to my second one either. In fact, I wasn't going to do anything but lie in the bed and be lazy. Well, at least until it was time for me to hook up with Jason.

Blackmailing Professor Reynolds to make sure that I got an A in his class wasn't enough. I had to get back at his ass for treating me like trash, and whether he knew it or not his son was gonna pay for his sins with his heart. Toi farted loudly causing me to wrinkle my nose up. Stankin' bitch. A sudden thought occurred to me. Why should I settle for embarrassing Professor Reynolds, when I could make the nigga pay me for my silence?

A large smile came across my face. The more I thought about the idea, the more I liked it. He was gonna pay in more ways than one for talking to me like I was one of them nothin' ass broads he was used to dealing with. I smiled sinisterly and fell back to sleep.

# # #

"Damn, that was a good ass nap," I said, stretching my limbs. My blurry sight became clear after I blinked a few times and wiped the matter from my eyes. My body felt rejuvenated. Sleep was just what I needed to refresh my mind and spirit. Now I could get on with the business at hand of making that bitch ass Professor bow down. I looked at the clock and was surprised to see that it was almost three o' clock in the afternoon.

"Damn," I mumbled to myself. "I was sleepy as fuck."

"You sho' was bitch," Toi said from the other side of the room. "Yo' ass was out for the count."

I sniffed the air and a familiar smell snaked through my nose. I got up and walked to the other side where Toi had blazed up a blunt.

"Damn, bitch you stay getting high," I told her.

"I guess that means you straight huh? You don't want none of the good kush."

"Shit, girl you better pass that shit," I said reaching for the happy grass.

"So what was up with you and that skinny nigga last night?"

"The fuck you mean what was up with him?" I asked in between puffs.

"Did y'all get busy or what?"

I looked at her like she'd lost her damn mind.

"Girl what the fuck you think? You think I'm gonna bring a nigga back to the crib and not sample his cock game?"

"Hey," she said throwing her hands up, "the only reason I asked was because when I came in the room this morning, you was in the bed alone."

I snickered and smiled. 'I might as well get this conversation over with now', I thought.

"What? Girl don't tell me that nigga's fuck game was pitiful," she said laughing.

"Nope. It was quite the opposite. It was pretty good. The nigga even tossed my salad, girl!"

"Bitch, quit lying," she said wide eyed.

"Girl, I'm tellin' you! That nigga licked my asshole so good, I fuckin' came!"

Toi giggled hard at the information that I'd just hit her with. Then after her giggling stopped, she looked at me with her head tilted to the side.

"Then what the hell are you snickering about?"

"Girl, that muthafucka got mad as fuck at me afterwards."

"What the fuck you do, Candice?"

"Well, I guess while we was fucking, I accidentally called him another nigga's name."

"What? Ah hell nah! Girl now you know that's some foul ass shit," she said laughing.

"I know girl. I felt bad about that shit at first, but then that nigga had the fucking nerve to act like he was catching feelings and shit. Talking about 'I thought you said you was single.' I was like nigga I am single, but what the fuck difference does it make to you? You got the pussy didn't you? Stop crying like a little bitch! That's when his ass got mad and left."

While Toi was busy laughing her ass off, I picked up my phone of the night stand and saw that Jason had called me twice and text me once. I quickly texted him back telling him that I had some things to take care of this morning, but I was free now if he wanted to get together.

"Who the fuck you texting?" She asked still cracking up.

I put my phone down, looked at her, and smiled. It was time to let my bff in on exactly what I planned on doing to get back at Professor Reynolds. After I told her, she called me an evil bitch, laughed some more, and then told me she had to get to her afternoon class. After she left, I jumped in the shower to get ready to meet Jason. Today I was going to meet him in the park and make my move. I knew that there was no way that he would be able to resist my charms. Once again, I put on one of the shortest miniskirts I could find. No panties, of course. My goal was to try to get him to finger fuck me and then take me back to his house so I could give him some of this pussy. After getting oiled up and dressed, I headed out the door. When I texted Jason, I told him that I would meet him at the same corner that he dropped me off at before. Letting him know where I lived was never a part of the plan. And it wasn't going to be either. By the time I got to there, Jason was just pulling up.

"Hey sexy lady," he said as he jumped out of the car and opened the door for me. He was very much a gentleman. A small part of me felt bad about what I was going to put him through, but fuck it. He was just a mean to an end.

"Thanks baby," I said as lustfully as I could.

After closing the door for me, he tried to look cool while walking back to the driver's side and turned too quickly, running right into the bumper as a result. I had to bend my head down to the floor and pretend that I had dropped something to keep from laughing at his clumsy ass. *'I hope this nigga can find the pussy when I decide to give it to his clumsy ass,'* I thought to myself.

"You ready baby?" He asked.

"Whenever you are, sweet thing."

When we got to the park, I looked down at Jason's lap and saw that he already had a hard on. This was going to be like taking candy from a fucking baby.

"Let's get out and walk around a little bit," I said, opening the door and getting out before he had a chance to object. Disappointment registered on his face as he got out of the driver's side. If this nigga thought he was about to fuck me in his raggedy ass car, he had another thing coming. Me and Jason walked slowly across the grass holding hands. His grip was warm and soft and almost made me feel bad about what I was going to do to him. Almost, but not quite. I was on a fuckin' mission to inflict some pain and nothing or no one was going to stand in my way. I looked around and tried to find an inconspicuous spot. I didn't want this nerdy muthafucka to get scared because he thought someone was looking at us. I spotted a bench to the far right and led him over to it. After sitting down next to him, I placed my hand on his thigh. Jason shuttered. It was obvious that he didn't get a lot of action with the ladies. This was good. The less experienced he was, the easier it was going to be for me to pussy whip his ass.

"Don't be nervous, baby. I won't bite unless you want me to."

He laughed a nerdy laugh as I ran my hand up his leg and touched his dick. Gently and slowly, I started squeezing it. It only took a few seconds for it to get hard again. I glanced up at Jason and saw that he'd closed his eyes. I grabbed the flap on his zipper and pulled it down. His dick struggled to get out. I looked back up at him and saw him look around like he was about to get caught by the principal.

"Wait...what if somebody sees us?" He stammered.

"Don't worry about it baby. If they want a show, we will damn sure give it to them."

"But I don't know if we should be …oh shit!" He said as I lowered my head down onto his pipe. "Damn, that shit feel good as fuck," he moaned.

For a nerd, Jason had a pretty decent sized dick. The shaft was smooth and clean and thicker than I thought it was. Knowing he probably couldn't take much more of my vacuum head, I stopped abruptly.

"What the fuck you doing? Why you stop?" He asked, breathing heavily.

"You're right baby," I said looking around as if I gave a fuck. "I'm starting to think people are going to see us too. I think we need to stop."

"What?? Ah hell nah baby, don't do that! Don't stop!"

"Well, if I'm going to finish you off, we need to go somewhere we won't be seen."

"Can we go back to your place?"

"Nah, my roommate is there," I lied.

Jason looked at me with a blank expression on his face. I could tell that he was trying to figure out where he could take me besides his house. When he hesitated a little too long, I decided to put a little pressure on him.

"You know. Maybe you should just take me home. I mean if we don't have anywhere to go where we can have some privacy, then this isn't going to work."

I started to get up and he grabbed my arm.

"Hold up. I know where we can go. We can go back to my place."

Before I even had a chance to answer him, Jason pulled me off the bench and towards the car. Jason sped through the streets so fast I thought we would crash on the way there. The car hadn't come to a full stop before he was jumping out of the driver's side. Before I knew it, he was on my side, opening the door and dragging me out. As soon as we got in the house, I ripped his shirt off. I wanted this nigga to know that he was dealing with a beast in bed. I took a quick glance around his house and saw a family portrait hanging on the wall. Professor Reynold's face stared out at us.

He wore a large smile on his face and stood behind someone whom I presumed to be his wife. Standing next to him was Jason. They all looked like one big happy family. I smiled on the inside, knowing that my revenge was going to be as sweet as ever. I sat down on the couch and reached for his belt buckle. After unbuckling it, I once again unzipped his zipper and stuck my hand inside of his pants. His dick damn near jumped out of his pants. It pointed at my face like a javelin. My pussy jumped like a pogo stick and dripped like a faucet. I leaned my head forward and stuck my tongue out, flicking it across the head of his penis. Jason trembled with delight. I don't know if he'd ever had his dick sucked before, but I was about to put something on his ass that he damn sure wasn't used to. After circling my tongue around it for about ten seconds, I slid my lips around it and let it glide over the shaft. My saliva dripped on the floor as I slurped his cum tool. Jason moaned out loud as I reached behind him and grabbed his ass cheeks.

"You ready baby? You ready to hit this pussy?" I asked him.

"Hell yeah baby! Let's hurry up and do this shit!"

I saw him sneak a peek at the clock. Apparently he wanted to hurry up and get done. If I had to guess it would be because he wanted me to be out of there before his mother or father got home. I was halfway tempted to keep fucking and sucking him until his one or the other came home, but I had a better plan for Professor Reynold's ass.

"Go get a condom baby. Yo do have one, right?"

I didn't know if he had one or not. I was just trying to get him to leave the room for a minute. That nigga ran up the steps so fast I thought he was going to break his leg on the way up. While he was gone, I quickly took my cell phone and placed it on the table. I maneuvered it so that it was facing the couch and punched the record function on the phone camera. Then, as fast as I could, I got out of my clothes. When Jason came back, he almost tripped over the couch when he saw my lusciousness.

"Damnnn," he whispered to himself.

"That's right baby, and it's all for you," I said as seductive as I can.

After lying back on the couch, I used my index finger and motioned for him to come towards me. That nigga's dick almost poked out of his pants.

"You ever ate pussy before, baby?" I asked him.

I was surprised when he shook his head from side to side. I thought that in this day and age everybody who was somebody dipped below the cunt line. I scratched that idea real quick. I didn't have time to teach some young buck how to eat pussy. Even though I was doing this to get back at Professor Reynold's, I did want to have some fun while doing it. "Well, don't worry about it baby. Let me show you how I get down."

I grabbed his dick, stuck it in my mouth, and started sucking it like it was a lollipop. Jason's whole body trembled. To my surprise, Jason had a pretty decent sized cock. When I first went for it at the park I thought I was going to sucking on something that resembled the lead sticking out of the end of pencil, but instead I was staring at the whole pencil. I lifted his rock hard member up and licked his balls while slowly stroking his dick. I glanced up at my phone and gave it a quick wink, knowing that everything we were doing was being recorded. After sucking Jason's dick for another couple of minutes, I pushed him back and threw my right leg over the back end of the couch. Then I pulled my left leg up to my shoulder, inviting him to my goodness.

"Come and get it baby."

Jason all but dove into the pussy. His dick filled me up much more than I thought it would. As he plunged in and out of me like a jack rabbit, I had a strong urge to tell this nigga to slow down. I hadn't had a muthafucka go in and out of me this fast since high school. I was sure he was going to come quick, but he didn't. He pumped for another ten minutes before filling the condom with juice. I looked my cell phone and smiled knowing that I had just done something that would really piss Professor Reynold's off.

Next Door Nympho 2

21

Candice

The next morning, I showed Toi the video that I'd shot.

"Damn bitch, that nigga knocking the stuffin' outta yo' pussy," Toi said, smirking. I ignored her smart assed-comment and continued watching, getting hotter by the minute. I never knew seeing yourself fuck on the screen was such a turn on. Although I did have Toi record the incident with Professor Reynolds, my hatred of his ass kept me from looking at it. I glanced at Toi's lips and immediately got wet. Ever since the threesome with her parents, I'd been wondering if Toi's pussy tasted as good as her mother's but I hadn't had the courage to act on it so far.

"So what you gon' do with this video?" Toi asked, interrupting my lewd thoughts of her.

I smiled wickedly.

"Well, at first I was going to show it to Professor Reynolds just to piss him off and complete my revenge. But since his son asked me to come over for dinner Friday night, I think I'll just show up and shock the fuck out of him," I said laughing.

Toi's mouth opened and her eyebrows shot up at the same time.

"That lil nigga invited you to dinner?"

"Yep."

Toi let out a low whistle.

"Girl, you better be careful playing wit' that lil nigga's heart like that. I can see you getting back at the

Professor for playing you like you was a cheap trick. But fuckin' wit' that lil nigga's feelings can get you fucked up."

I looked at this bitch like she was crazy. If I didn't know better I would think this hoe was getting soft.

"What? Girl fuck that lil nigga. I'll bitch slap his ass into next week if he fucks with me."

I looked at the clock and saw that it was almost time for me to go to Professor Reynold's class. After talking with Toi a few more minutes, I made my way out the door and over to his classroom. As soon as I walked in, Professor Reynolds shot me a sly look. I wanted to cuss his ass out so bad I could barely stand it. The smug look he gave me almost caused me to flip out. It took everything in me not to snatch out my cell phone, walk up to his desk, and show him the picture of me fucking his son. This muthafucka thought he had gotten what he wanted from me and fucked me over, but I had a trick coming for his ass.

"Damn, girl, where you been?" One of my classmates asked me. I simply shrugged my shoulders without answering her. *'Damn, these bitches are nosey as fuck,'* I thought to myself. All during class I kept a straight face while Professor Reynolds walked around the room and talked with the confidence of a man that had just gotten away with something. But I definitely had a trick or two up my sleeve. With hatred in my eyes, I stared at him. When class was over, I just sat there burning a hole through his ass.

"Miss Robinson, you can leave now. Class is over and I have more important things to do than sit up here and listen to you ramble about some non-sense. Get out!"

I smiled as I got up out of my seat and walked, looking back at him every now and then. I wanted to throw the video in his face but dinner at his house was going to be so much more satisfying. I gave him a devilish grin as I left. The more I walked the more I thought about how I didn't want to wait until Friday to fuck him up. I hopped on my cell phone and called Jason. His ass was so happy to hear from me I swear that I could almost see his ass smiling through the phone.

"Hey, I forgot that I had an appointment on Friday. We're gonna have to have dinner another time," I said, hoping that he would panic and move the dinner date up. It worked like a charm. It took Jason all of three seconds to invite me to dinner tonight. I couldn't wait to get to his house so I can fuck Professor Reynold's head all the way up. I strolled into my dorm's building and walked in. Tonight, I was going to wear the sexiest thing I had in my repertoire. Check that. I was going to wear the sluttiest thing I had in my repertoire. When the professor took one look at me, his dick was going to get so hard, he wouldn't be able to stand up without punching a hole in his pants. I smiled as I got off the elevator and made my way towards my room door. The closer I got to the door, the more my ears perked up. My hot box got moist as I heard Toi moaning through the door. Carefully I eased the door open. I tiptoed in slowly and slid to the right. Craning my neck, I got a full view of Toi's naked body. It was beautiful. Her legs were spread eagle as she laid on her back and finger fucked herself. Toi was so into it, she never even knew I was there. Heat shot through my body as her face twisted into a mask of pleasure. My thoughts raced back to the threesome I'd had with Toi's parents. The more I thought about how her mother ate me out the more I wondered how Toi's tongue would feel. Not wanting to embarrass her, I eased back out of the door. I just stood there for a few seconds wondering what she would do if I walked back in, got into bed with her, and started licking her clit. I quickly shook my head from side to side. *'What the fuck am I thinking about? I'm not a fuckin' dyke.'* I opened the door, walked back in, and slammed it. Apparently, Toi didn't give a fuck about that. She finger banged herself for another ten seconds before exploding all over her bed. Then she jumped up like it was no big deal. I guess it wasn't though. If I was jacking the fuck off, I wouldn't let anyone stop me from getting a nut either.

"Damn, that shit felt good as fuck," she said on her way to the bathroom.

"Damn girl, you couldn't find you no real meat today?"

"Bitch please," she said. "You know damn well I can get dick any time I want it."

"Then what the fuck you doing in here playing with ya fuckin' self for?"

"Cause I didn't feel like being bothered with some punk ass nigga," she said. "Don't get me wrong now. I love dick just as much as the next bitch, but today is just one of those days where I don't feel like being bothered with anybody other than myself."

I just shook my head and laughed as Toi threw on her bathrobe and walked toward the bathroom. I didn't have anything else planned for the day, so I figured that I would just lie around, relax, fuck around on face book, and take a nap until it was time for the date.

# # #

A satisfied smile came across my face as I looked in the mirror to confirm what I already knew. I was one sexy bitch. I blew myself a kiss and twirled around to get a better look. My plump, juicy ass was curved perfectly as it rested underneath the thigh high mini-skirt I chose to wear.

I wanted to lick my lips but decided not to for fear of sweeping away the glittered lip gloss I had so carefully applied. My titties were perky and my blouse was tight. My makeup was also flawless and my legs were downright mesmerizing as I slipped my painted toenails into my high heeled pumps. I was going to fuck Professor Reynolds up with this move. I almost bust a nut visualizing the look on his face when I showed up at his house on his son's arm. That nigga was going to shit a brick. After looking at myself in the mirror a couple more times to make sure that I was indeed fly as fuck, I headed out the door. I thought it was weird that Jason and his family were having dinner so early. It was barely four o' clock but since I was getting free grub as well as sweet revenge, I wasn't going to complain. It was kind of warm so I decided against wearing a jacket. Besides, that would hinder some of my sex appeal. Heads turned and jaws dropped as I made my way up the sidewalk. Jason was a little upset at first when I told him that we would have to meet at the convenient store on the corner, but I quickly fixed that by lying to him and telling him that my dorm room had to be fumigated. Shit, I'd be a fool to let him know where I lived. The last thing I needed was for this clingy ass nigga to start hanging around stalking me after I dumped his ass. When I got to the store he hadn't arrived yet, so I went into the store and bought a pack of gum. After paying for my purchase, I looked up and saw Jason pulling into the parking lot.

"Showtime," I mumbled to myself as I walked towards the door. As I left, I heard someone say "Damn baby, you fine as fuck."

"You damn right I am," I shot back as I strutted out of the store without even looking back. Jason was all smiles as he walked around the car and opened the door for me.

"Thanks baby," I said, giving him a gentle peck on the lips. Stealing a glance at his crotch as I slid into the car, I noticed that he was already rock hard. I thought about giving him a blow job on the way to his house but I didn't want him to crash and kill us.

"I can't wait for you to meet my parents," he said, pulling out of the parking lot and into the flow of traffic.

"I can't wait either, baby. What did you say your father did again?" I asked, feigning ignorance.

"Oh, he's a Professor at the college. And my mother works for the post office."

Once again I looked down at his hard on. The shit was making me hot as fuck. I reached over and grabbed his right hand and guided it between my legs.

"Why you doing?" he said excitedly.

"Just giving a sample of what you're gonna get later on…if you're a good boy," I said teasing him. I slowly spread my legs and eased his middle finger into my sweet cave. After pumping it in and out for a few seconds, I took it out and stuck it into my mouth. You should've seen this niggas face while I was doing this. I thought he was gonna bust a nut in his pants right then. As a matter of fact, if we hadn't drove up to his house I'm sure he would have. Jason parked and I reached for the door only to have him yell out.

"Wait!" he screamed as he jumped out of the car and ran around to open the door for me. "Let a true gentleman get that for you baby." This guy was making all the right moves. It's a shame that I was going to have break his heart. I was so focused on screwing him the last time I was here, I hadn't taken the time to notice how nice their house was. It was a very large brick colonial with neatly trimmed grass. The driveway was long and wide with an attached two car garage. A giant tree rested in the yard surrounded by brown mulch. On both sides of the house were two pretty flower beds, with roses growing out of one side and petunias growing out of the other.

"You gonna walk in the house like that?" I asked looking down at his hard on again. Jason stopped in his tracks. I guess he hadn't thought about what his parents were going to say when he strolled in with his dick trying to poke its way out of its denim cage. After a few seconds, he shrugged his shoulders.

"Fuck it," he said softly. "Ain't nothin' I can do about it now."

Jason reached into his pocket and pulled out his keys. Upon entering the house, I looked to the left and saw the couch that I had fucked Jason's brains out on. It gave me a perverse sense of pleasure. I turned my head back and saw one of the most beautiful women that I had ever seen in my life. She had fair brown skin and soft, brown deep set eyes. Her smile radiated the room along with shallow dimples that highlighted her features. Her hair was perfect. There wasn't a strand of it out of place. The way she walked towards us made me think that she used to be a model or something.

"So, you're the young lady my son keeps bragging about," she said in a low alto toned voice that turned even me on. I looked at Jason and then back at his mother. It had never occurred to me that Jason had been talking to his mother about me. The thought suddenly popped into my mind that he'd mentioned my name a time or two. "So, what's your name young lady?" she asked, squashing my fears. "For some reason, my son didn't mention your name." I silently thanked God for my lucky break. I could've kicked myself in the ass for giving Jason my real name. But after tonight, it won't matter.

"Candice," I said as sheepishly as I could. I wanted her to think that I was as innocent as a new born baby.

"Well, Candice let me show you to the restroom so you can wash your hands."

"Thank you," I said as she led me to their bathroom. After washing my hands, I came out of the bathroom to find her standing there waiting on me. She then led me to the dining room area where the scintillating smell of food quickly swam through my nose. My stomach immediately started growling. The sweat aroma reminded me that I hadn't eaten anything except a fish sandwich all day. Not only was I going to rub the fact that I was fuckin' Professor Reynolds' son in his face, I was going to eat his ass out of house and home. I looked at the table and the food caused my mouth to water. There was Pork Roast, Corn Bread, Mashed Potatoes, Macaroni and Cheese, Cream Spinach, and a large pitcher of Iced Tea. As I entered the room, Jason got up and quickly walked around the table. He almost sprained his arm trying to pull the chair out for me. His mother giggled and shook her head. Apparently she thought it was amusing that her son was head over hills in love with a Goddess. A slow and devious smile crept onto my face as I heard the sound of a garage door open. I could have sworn I felt a drop of cum ooze down my leg. Once I heard a door slam I was sure of it.

"That's my husband. He'll be in here in a few seconds. We usually have dinner around this time. We believe that the family that eats together, stays together," she said.

"I'll be in there in a second, honey," I heard the Professor say. "Just let me wash my hands."

"Hurry up honey. I want you to meet Jason's friend."

I sat there quietly in anticipation of Professor Reynolds coming into the dining room. This was a moment I was going to savor. Although I know it was just a few seconds, it seemed to take an hour for him to bring his snake ass into the room.

"Sorry I'm late. I had to…" Professor Reynolds stopped dead in his tracks. The look on his face when he saw me was worth a thousand words. Jason's mother got up and walked over to him.

"I know honey," she said, giving him a peck on the cheek. "I felt the same way when I saw her. Couldn't believe our son could snag such a beautiful young lady."

Sweat popped up on the Professors head. His right eye twitched. I was sure that he was struggling to keep from pissing in his pants. Jason's mother walked back over to the table to sit down, while her shell shocked husband continued to stand there looking stupid. After a few seconds, Professor Reynolds walked over to the table and eased his scared ass into the chair.

"Jason, say grace," his mother told him. "Everybody bow their heads please." As Jason was saying grace, I slowly opened my eyes and looked at the Professor. I gave him a devilish smirked as he looked at me like he wanted to commit murder. Just before Jason said amen, I blow his simple ass a kiss. Throughout the dinner, I reveled in the fact that I could blow his ass out of the water. The rest of us engaged in light conversation, while the Professor remained rather quiet. He looked like he wanted to shit on himself. Just then, their house phone rang.

"Excuse me," Jason's mother said, getting up to go answer the phone. The second she walked out, the Professor started trying to get rid of Jason.

"Hey son. Why don't you go get the photo album so we can show your "girlfriend" some pictures of you when you were younger." It took everything in me to keep me from laughing in his face. He was upset as hell, and I'm sure he was going to let me know just how much as soon as Jason got out of the room.

"What the fuck are you doing in my house?" he seethed.

"As you said, Professor, I'm your son's new girlfriend," I smirked. "Hmmm, I wonder if you son's dick tastes as good as yours?" I said, as if I had never fucked him before. "But then again, I may have already fucked him," I said, giving him some food for thought. Professor Reynolds' light skin turned a darker shade of red.

"Bitch! If you don't stay the fuck away from my son I'll…"

"You ain't gonna do a muthafuckin' thing. And you want to know why you ain't gonna do shit?" I asked him, speaking ghetto like my girl Toi. I got up out of my seat and walked around to where he was sitting, taking my cell phone out along the way. "Watch this muthafucka," I said, holding it up to his face. I quickly put it into record mode and pressed play. Turning the volume down I gave the Professor a front row seat for the porn movie I'd made with is son. His mouth almost dropped on the floor. The way he was looking at my phone told me that he wanted to snatch it out of my hand and smash it into a thousand pieces. "And just in case you're thinking about taking my phone from me and breaking it, I've uploaded it to my laptop," I told him as I walked back to my seat.

"Dad I don't know why you told me to go get these embarrassing pictures," Jason said as he returned to the room. Two seconds after Jason returned, his mother came back in.

"Sorry about that everyone. That was my mother honey." She looked at the photo album with a raised eyebrow. "Okay, which one of you had the idea to go and get that album?" She asked, looking at the Professor suspiciously.

"Hey, dad told me to go and get it. You know good and well I wouldn't have done that crap."

"Really?" she asked, raising her eyebrows even higher. "You usually hate looking at those pictures." The Professor just shrugged his shoulders. "Are you okay dear? You look like you've been sweating. It's not even hot in here. I hope you're not getting sick," she said as she walked over to him and felt his forehead.

"I'm fine," he said, pushing her hand away. "Let's eat."

Throughout the entire dinner, I made it a nightmare for Professor Reynolds. I couldn't touch Jason enough. Every so often I would lean over and give him a kiss. I know it must have really made his blood boil when his wife was telling us how good a couple we made. I thought I saw a tear leak from the side of his eye when I told Jason that he's the type of man that I'd love to marry one day. It felt so good that I planned to fuck Jason's brains out as soon as we left his house. By the end of the evening, Professor Reynold's was snapping at everyone, including his wife.

"What the hell is wrong with you?" she asked him.

"Nothing. I just have a headache."

"Well, I've really enjoyed having dinner with you all, bit I have a busy day ahead of me tomorrow. Jason, could you take me home please?" I asked him batting my eyes seductively.

As I stood up too from the table, Jason's mother walked around it. She opened her arms and invited me into a loving embrace. For one brief moment, a twinge of guilt washed over me. Then I remembered how much I despised her husband and quickly swatted that ridiculous feeling to the side.

"It was nice meeting you," she said with a pleasant smile. "Maybe we can have you over for dinner again one day.

"That would be nice, especially if things work out between me and Jason," I said taking one last jab at the Professor. I smiled at Jason and, when I was sure that no one was looking, shot a devious wink to Professor Reynolds. He was so mad, I could almost feel the heat radiating from his temper.

"For heaven's sake dear, give Jason's friend a hug. Let her know that you were glad to meet her. Where are your manners?" She admonished him. This woman was being so nice to me, that I once again almost felt bad. Almost.

"Oh I'm sorry Felicia," he said calling his wife by her first name. Where are my manners? Professor Reynolds grabbed me by the shoulders and pulled me in close. To the casual eye it probably looked like a harmless jester, but the professor squeezed the hell out of me when he hugged me. It was obvious that he was trying to cause me pain and discomfort.

"Watch it, muthafucka," I whispered in his ear.

"I'm gonna get you for this, bitch," he mumbled through gritted teeth.

"Don't count on it. Now let me go nigga." The professor released me and stared at me with eyes that revealed a coldness that made me shiver.

"I'm sure that things will work out just fine for you and Jason. As it will for all of us," he spat.

Jason's mother said goodbye to me once more and started clearing dishes from the table.

"I'll be back in a few. I'm about to drive Candice home right quick," Jason told his dad. When Jason's mother went into the kitchen, I leaned in close to him and thanked him again for inviting me to dinner. Then I did the unthinkable. When I was sure that his father was looking, I grabbed Jason's dick and gave it a gentle squeeze. Jason's mouth fell open as his head snapped around towards his father. Not wanting to embarrass his son, the professor quickly turned his head. Without saying a word, Jason grabbed me by the hand and started pulling me towards the door. I looked back at Professor Reynolds one last time, licking my lips and giving him some food for thought about what I was going to do for his son.

Next Door Nympho 2

22

Candice

Getting my revenge on Professor Reynold's felt so good, I nearly came on myself. The look on that muthafuckas face was priceless. That'll teach his ass to fuck with a superstar bitch like me.

"So, did you enjoy yourself today?" Jason asked.

"More than you know baby, more than you know," I said, sliding my hand between his legs. I was so amped up I wanted to make him pull over give him a blow job right then and there. Since we were only a few minutes away from the park, I decided that it would be smarter and more comfortable to go there. My pussy was on fire and Jason's dick was just the extinguisher I needed. His dick grew through his pants. In a matter of seconds it resembled a piece of steel. There was no use in letting a hard one go to waste, so I figured I might as well get me some before I dumped his ass.

"Damn baby, you hard as fuck," I said as I unzipped his pants, reached inside, and messaged his tool. "Let's stop off at the park so I can…"

Before I could finish my sentence, my cell phone rang. I started to not answer it, but something inside of me told me that it might be important. I frowned as I looked at the screen and saw that it was Toi's worrisome ass. Knowing that if I didn't answer, she would just keep calling back, I pushed the answer button.

"What's up Toi?" I annoyingly asked.

"Hey girl. Whatever you're doing, you need to drop it and come home. A package came for you today that I think you are gonna wanna check out." *A package?* I thought.

"Toi what the hell are you talking about?"

"Bitch, I just told you what the fuck I'm talking about. Look, just hurry up and bring yo' ass home or I'ma take care of this package myself."

Now she had me curious. As much as I wanted some dick, I just had to know what the hell this mysterious package was. I looked over at Jason, who seemed to pick up on the fact that he wasn't going to get any nookie this night.

"I'm sorry boo. But I need you to take me home."

"What's wrong?" he asked.

"Some kind of emergency at my place. My roommate didn't want to talk about it over the phone. She just said she needed me to come home."

I had Jason drop me off at an apartment building about three blocks from my dorm.

"Oh, so this is where you stay huh?"

"Yep," I lied to him with a straight face.

"You want me to walk you in?" he asked as he turned the car off and began to get out.

"No, I'm good," I said, grabbing his arm to prevent it.

"Damn girl, when you gonna let a brother visit?"

"I'll call you tomorrow baby." It was a lie as soon as it left my mouth. I had no intentions of calling him tomorrow. As far as I was concerned, his services were no longer required. He was now useless. The next time I talked to him, it would be to tell him that we were through. I walked into the building's lobby and glanced back. He was still staring at me as I made my way to the elevator. I stood there, waiting for him to pull off. As soon as he did, I ran out the door and made my way down the street. My mind was working overdrive to try and figure out what surprise awaited me in my dorm room. On my way there, I decided to twist the knife into Professor Reynold's back just a little deeper. I took my cell phone out and texted him the video of me sucking Jason's dick. After looking at it a few times, I memorized the bastard's cell number by heart so instead of going to my contact list, I just pressed his number in. I also felt that it was about time I let his ass know that I had our little fuck session on file as well. After sending the message, I smiled and waited for him to call back and cuss me out. Like I would really give a fuck. When the call didn't come, I just shrugged it off and kept stepping. As I entered my dorm's lobby, I thought I heard someone calling me but I wasn't sure. But instead of turning around to see if I was just hearing things, I kept walking. The suspense of the surprise was killing me. I hopped on the elevator and rode up. After arriving at my floor, I got off and power walked my way down to my dorm room. I inserted the key into the lock, opened the door, and gasped. Lying on my bed in all his splendor was Rashawn. My pussy instantly did a somersault. My mouth watered. I looked at Toi, who stared at me with a devious grin.

"Surprise," she said.

"Rashawn! When did you get here?"

"About an hour ago. I's been awhile since we hooked up so I figured I would come down here and check you out, sweet thing."

'An hour? This nigga has been here an hour and this bitch is just now calling me? What the fuck have they been doing in that time? I know she said that they were old

friends but this bitch like dick just as much as I do,' I thought. I sniffed the air a couple of times trying to see if I detected the smell of sex.

"Bitch please," Toi said, knowing exactly what I was thinking. "I told yo' ass before it ain't even like that." Rashawn looked at me, then at Toi, obviously confused. Before anyone could say anything else, there was a knock at the door. Toi walked past me and opened it. She didn't seem to be surprised that someone was visiting us. When she opened the door, I was shocked to see her parents standing there smiling.

"Hey. I was wondering when you guys would get here," Toi said.

Toi's parents looked at Rashawn and then at Toi. They were probably wondering if he was there to see Toi or me. I put an end to that line of thinking when I waltzed over to him, sat down beside him, and hugged him tightly.

"Me and my parents are about to go out to dinner. I hope you like the surprise I left for you," she said with a wicked grin.

"Oh, I'm sure I will," I purred.

"What surprise? I thought she was coming with us," her father said, disappointed. He probably couldn't wait to get another taste of this juicy pussy. I couldn't blame him though. My coochie was the bomb.com.

"No, you guys go ahead. I'm going to stay here and chill with my friend. I'm sure we can find something to do while y'all gone."

"Yes, I'm sure you will," Toi's mother said with a hint of sarcasm in her voice. I couldn't wait for the three of them to leave so I can do what I do best, which is fuck a nigga's brains out. As soon as they left the room, I reached for Rashawn's dick. I couldn't wait for him to put it in my mouth. My pussy dripped as he unzipped his pants and pulled out his huge python. I don't know if this nigga was just blessed or deformed as hell but he had the biggest dick I'd ever seen. No wonder I'd been having wet dreams about his ass. My mouth had a mind of its own. It seemed to dive towards his crotch. I spread my jaws wide and let it slide smoothly into my throat. This muthafucka's dick was so big, it was in my throat and I could still see some of the shaft. I swear if he didn't have eleven inches, he didn't have an inch. I struggled to keep from gagging while Rashawn's huge monster tunneled through my throat. Rashawn placed his hand on top of my head and tried to force his dick into my lungs. My eyes watered. This nigga was severely testing my gag reflex. Even though I was choking, I was still supremely turned on by what was happening. I pulled Rashawn's hand off of my head and came up for air. If I didn't know any better, I would swear that his cock had grown another inch and a half since the last time he pounded my love hole.

"What's wrong down there baby?" he asked smugly.

"Shit, nigga ain't nothing wrong. I love this dick." A satisfied smile fell across his face when I admitted to him what we both had already known.

"I guess you don't wanna stop suckin' it then huh?" he asked, starting to stuff it back into his pants.

"Hell no," I said, grabbing it and putting it back into my mouth. "I want to suck the shit out of it." I blew him for another five minutes before standing up and taking off my clothes. Rashawn did the same. I thought about turning on some music so the other residents wouldn't hear me screaming out in ecstasy, but then figured fuck it. The rest of them hoes would probably be jealous any damn way. My pussy was so wet, it was sticking to my panties as I pulled them off. I crawled into bed and spread my legs wide. I took a deep breath as Rashawn crawled between them. Thankfully, he took mercy on me and eased the head in instead of jamming the whole thing in. Rashawn stopped for a brief moment and coughed out loud a couple of time but I know he wasn't going to let that stop him from diving into this golden pussy. Inch by beautiful inch, Rashawn pushed his tool into my warm hole. With each passing second I got closer and closer to sex heaven. Then, all of a sudden he started withdrawing his deposit. My eyes popped open only to see him smirking at me.

"Nigga what the fuck you doing? Put that muthafucka back in!" Rashawn laughed lightly and proceeded to push the head back in. But once again, when he got halfway to hitting my sweat spot, he pulled out. I opened my eyes again, but this time they were filled with anger. This nigga was playing with my orgasm and I didn't like the shit one bit. I was well aware of the fact that he was teasing me in an attempt to heighten the intensity of the moment, but fuck that! I wanted some dick and I wanted it now!

"Mutahfucka quit playing!" I yelled. The smile that was previously on Rashawn's face disappeared. His eyes narrowed into slits.

"Bitch who the fuck you think you talkin' to like that? You wanna get fucked? Okay bitch, you about to get fucked!"

Rashawn grabbed my legs and pushed them back over my head. From the look on his face I was in for the fuck of my life. I braced myself as he leaned forward so my legs were resting on his shoulders and slammed inside of me. Now I know my pussy is deep, but just like last time, he was touching spots that were reserved for surgeons. I swear, this nigga was in my stomach.

"Oh shit, baby I'm sorry," I screamed, hoping that he would ease up on my womb. This muthafucka was banging the juice out of my pussy. "Oh my God, Rashawn, please take it easy!"

"Shut up bitch! You wanted this dick, now you gon' get this muthafucka!"

In the process of really trying to punish my coochie, Rashawn reared back and got ready to deliver the death stroke. Luckily for me, his dick slipped out, giving me temporary relief from his assault. It was short lived however, as some kind of way his dick had made its way to my ass hole opening. For the first time in my life, I was actually afraid of the dick. I saw a sinister smile on his face and knew exactly what he was thinking. I grabbed a glass that was sitting on the table next to my bed and looked at him.

"Nigga yo' ass better not!" I swear to God that if he woulda stuck that monster in my asshole, I was going to smash him in the head with that glass.

"I ain't gonna do you like that baby. I'm doing enough damage."

He wasn't lying. He was cutting a path through my pussy that I don't think another man could follow behind. I don't know if he all of a sudden felt sorry for me or what, but when he put it back in he was no longer trying to give me a hysterectomy. Don't get me wrong, I still felt every inch of him but it was immensely pleasurable. Rashawn started rotating his hips clockwise. He was hitting my sweet spots consistently and I was loving him for it. I wrapped my arms and my legs around him and begged him to give me more. It was even better than it was the first time.

"Oooo God baby, I'm about to come," I yelled.

Apparently telling him that I was about to bust one turned him on. Without trying to hurt me, he dug deeper, but with passion instead of anger. I saw spots as I erupted all over him and onto the bed sheets. Rashawn didn't stop. He continued to hit my spots. His sweet dick had me ready to come again. I tried to hold it as long as I could. I didn't want to come twice before he'd even come once, but I just couldn't help it. Three minutes after my first orgasm, I released my second one. Rashawn still hadn't came yet. Just as I was getting ready to submit and tell him that I couldn't take any more, he exploded inside of me. I hope these fucking birth control pills I'm taking works because Rashawn just poured a river of semen inside of me. I know we should have used a condom, but once we got started I forgot all about making him strap up. I thought I heard a few giggles outside of my door, but I didn't give a fuck. I was in heaven. This nigga had only fucked me twice, but he was fast making me fall in love with his ass.

# # #

After getting my pussy pounded a second time that night, I asked Rashawn if he wanted to spend the night. Even though I was completely drained, I still had to fight the urge to suck his dick in the middle if the night. After pushing my desires to the side, I fell asleep with my head on his chest. The sunshine came through the window the next morning and served as my alarm clock. I blinked twice trying to clean the sleep from my eyes while Rashawn snored lightly. My energy renewed, I looked down at his crotch and licked my lips. *'Damn bitch, you need to chill out. You're starting to act like a fucking nymphomaniac,'* I told myself silently. But my lips wouldn't listen to me. They betrayed me as they made their way down south. My mouth opened automatically. I reached down and took hold of his black garden hose hoping that I could get it to spring a leak by the time I was done. My tongue shot out like a snake descending on its prey and swiped back and forth against the mushroomed head. I glanced back at Rashawn as he stirred a bit. I gently sucked the head in a swift motion. Then I engulfed it with my mouth as it tickled the back of my tonsils. Up and down I went on his pole until Rashawn woke up.

"Damn, girl what you doing down there?" he asked groggily.

"I was hungry, baby."

"Well shit, girl don't let me stop you from eating." Rashawn grabbed a handful of my hair as I worked on the dick. Wanting to taste him, I increased my speed.

"Oh fuck! That's it girl, suck that muthafucka!" Spurred on by his nasty talk, I cupped his balls and messaged them. I moaned and sucked at the same time. It didn't take long for Rashawn to fill my belly with his seeds.

"Oh shit, swallow that shit girl! Swallow all that cum!" Rashawn didn't have to tell me twice. By the time he'd finished his sentence, I had gulped all of his babies down. We laid there for another thirty minutes before we got up and got cleaned up. Rashawn told me that he was hungry and decided that we should go get some breakfast.

"I hope you know a good place out here where to get some good grub at. A nigga hungry as fuck."

"I got you baby. I know a slamming ass pancake spot."

"That's what's up," he said rubbing his hands together. "Yo' I didn't bring a change of clothes, so I hope this ain't one of them uppity ass restaurants."

"Nah, baby the place is cool." I said reassuring him.

As we walked out of my dorm room, a couple of girls down the hall looked at me and snickered. I took that shit as a compliment. While I was in my room getting supremely satisfied, these hoes was probably wishing they were in my position. Homely looking bitches. I walked out of the dorm with a smile on my face. Them tramps probably went back to their rooms and jacked the fuck off. Me? I was getting ready to enjoy breakfast after having one of the best orgasms that I'd ever had in my life. Well, actually two. A sudden thought came to my mind. While leaving the room, I didn't see or hear Toi snoring from the other side of the room. I'm not even sure if she was there. I'll have to remember to call and thank her for not interrupting my flow. There was a light breeze blowing but it didn't affect me in the least. I was still warm from the hot sex I'd enjoyed with Rashawn. We entered Sandy's Pancake House and waited to be seated. Luckily they had a corner booth in the back of the place so me and Rashawn could quite possibly do some freaky shit if we so desired. I don't what the fuck the waitresses problem was, but on at least three occasions while she was leading us to ours booth, she would glance back and smile at Rashawn. I quickly grabbed Rashawn's hand to let her know to keep her slutty thoughts in her fucking head. I glared at her as we sat down. *'Look at me, acting like a jealous ass girlfriend',* I thought to myself. Apparently she got the hint as she pulled her gaze away from Rashawn and took our orders. While we were waiting for the flirty bitch to bring us our food, Rashawn kept telling me over and over how he was feeling me and how good my pussy was. Hell, I already knew that, but it was flattering to hear it from someone else's mouth. No sooner had Rashawn got up to go to the bathroom, our food arrived. The waitress seemed to be a bit disappointed that he wasn't there. She looked at the empty spot where he was sitting and sighed.

"Is there a problem?" I asked her, becoming increasingly annoyed that she didn't want to acknowledge that I was with him.

"Excuse me?"

"I asked you if there was a problem."

"No. why would you asked that?"

"Because you keep staring at my man like you've lost your fucking mind." Normally I didn't talk shit to a waitress for fear of what they would do to my food in the back. But this bitch was getting on my nerves. The woman stared at me for a minute before giving me a fake smile and setting our food down. She tried to stare me down as she walked away. I would have paid anything for that bitch to trip and fall. I was so busy mean mugging her ass, I hadn't noticed that Rashawn had gotten back.

"Everything ok?" he asked, seeing the look on my face.

"Yeah. Why you ask?"

"Cause you look like you getting ready to go gangsta on that waitress."

"Oh do I? Nah, everything good."

Time flew as we ate and conversed. I guess I didn't realize how hungry I was until I started eating. After devouring my stack of pancakes, I was more than ready for a second helping. Rashawn must have been as hungry as I was. He was mauling his eggs and home fries.

"So when are you leaving?" I asked, hoping that he would stay another day. At that moment, it occurred to me that I knew very little about this man. I didn't know where or if he worked. I didn't know his last name. Hell, I couldn't even remember if we had went to his house or his friend Malcom's the first time we'd hooked up. But I did know one important thing. This nigga's name shoulda been Rotor Router because her sure as hell knew how to lay the pipe.

"Damn girl, you trying to get rid of a nigga already?" he asked half smiling at me.

"Hell nah baby. On the contrary. I was hoping that you would stay another night."

Rashawn rubbed his chin. The mere fact that he was thinking about it had my panties moist. My clit thumped in anticipation of Rashawn's thick meat penetrating me once again.

"So you want me to stick around a little longer and tap that ass some more huh?"

I opened my mouth to say what we both already knew but the words stopped in my throat. My smile evaporated as soon as I looked across the room. Standing in the doorway with a dusty looking bitch on his arm was none other than Byron's punk ass. He was smirking at me and even had the nerve to blow a kiss in my direction. The bitch he was with was either blind as hell or chose to ignore it. Either way, the hoe looked retarded. Rashawn's eye followed me as I mean mugged the hell out of Byron.

"Who the fuck is this clown?" Rashawn asked.

"Just some muthafucka I used to date. I broke it off with his ass and now he wants to cause a scene every time he sees me. Let's go," I said standing up, getting ready to leave.

"The fuck you doin' ma? I thought you wanted some more pancakes?"

"I did. But seeing this muthafucka done spoiled my fucking appetite."

"Sit down! Fuck that nigga!" Rashawn said loud enough for Byron and his bitch to hear. "If you want some more food, then order some more food! If that nigga want a problem, I'll damn sure give his ass one!"

I eased back down, giddy at the fact that Rashawn was ready to throw down to defend my honor.

"Thanks bae," I said, smiling at him.

"It's all good. That nigga betta just stay in his fuckin' lane."

Listening to him put his thug voice down made me want Rashawn even more. At this point I seriously considered dragging him into the ladies bathroom and blowing his head. My thoughts, however, were interrupted by my vibrating cell phone. I looked at the screen and saw that I had a text message from Toi.

'Damn bitch, where u at? When I got home u and ol' boy was cuddled up and snoring like two lovers. I had a class this morning but when I got back y'all had got ghost. Hit me up when u get a chance and let me know you cool.'

I was loving my BFF right about now. Not only had she been a good friend since she got on campus, she'd also hooked me up with Rashawn's sweet dick ass.

"Aye yo' you gon' have to tell yo' boyfriend to stop texting you when you hanging out with a real nigga," Rashawn said, half laughing once again.

"Boy please. That wasn't nobody but Toi."

Once again we were enjoying each other's company so much that I'd almost forgotten that Byron was even in the place. Right on cue, he walked by and made his presence felt like I suspected he would, causing trouble in the process.

"Damn girl, you sho look different with yo' clothes on," he said insulting me. Before I had a chance to say anything back, Rashawn stood up. His large frame towered over Byron.

"Look here my dude. I don't know what went down between you and her and I really don't give a fuck. But you need to take yo' ass on before you end up getting fucked up!"

"Nigga you ain't gon' fuck nobody up! Fuck you and this dry pussy having hoe!"

"Nigga what you say?"

"You heard what the fuck I…"

Ummph!

The punch came so fast, Byron had virtually no time to react. Before he could even think of defending himself, he was doubled over from a hard shot to the gut. Rashawn followed that up with a two piece upper cut that put Byron flat on his back.

"Baby, you ok?" the girl he was with screamed as she rushed to his side. She leaned down and tried to comfort Byron as he lay on the floor, semi-conscious. "Nigga what the fuck wrong with you?" she asked as she got up and took a step towards Rashawn. But I was more than ready for this hoe. I stepped between her and Rashawn, ready to fuck her up if need be.

"Bitch you better back you're ugly ass up before you catch a headache!" By this time, the manager had made his way over and was threatening to call the police on us if we didn't get out.

"Let's roll the fuck up outta here," Rashawn spat. "This fuckin' place ain't all that." As we step past Byron, I made sure to 'accidently' step on his hand on the way out.

"Fuckin' bitch! You and that punk ass nigga gon' pay for that shit!" We ignored him and kept on stepping. I put an extra switch in my walk just to show Byron what he would never get again. The entire episode had me hot as a firecracker. The second we got inside Rashawn's car, I reached for his zipper. I was ready to stuff my jaws and didn't want to wait until I got back to the dorm room.

"That shit made me so fucking hot! Baby I need some cum!" A large smile crossed his face as I kissed the head. "I want you to take me back to my dorm room and fuck the shit out of me!"

"That's what the fuck I'm talking about baby! Bitch ass nigga Byron. I shoulda stomped on his fuckin' head before we left."

"Fuck that nigga," I said, lowering my mouth onto his dick.

Next Door Nympho 2

23

Unknown

"Would you like another glass of Orange Juice?" the waitress asked. The condescending tone she said it in led me to believe the bitch was trying to be funny. I'd had an uneventful night and didn't feel like hearing a bunch of bullshit. I also didn't feel like being bothered with anyone, which is why I chose a seat way back in the back of the restaurant where barely anyone could see me. If I was on the run from someone, all I had to do was come here and sit in this seat.

"Well, since you asked so fuckin' nicely I think I will take another one. A large glass this time."

The waitress smacked her lips and walked away. If she was having a bad day, that was just too damn bad. That shit wasn't my problem. When I got ready to order something to eat, I would and this bitch wasn't going to rush me. While she was getting my juice, I was going over my plan in my head. Even though everything was going according to plan, there was no telling when that bitch Charmaine would fuck it all up. I was starting to think that I was going to have to take care of her ass before she could. The waitress set the glass down on the table so hard, the juice almost spilled onto it. *'Yeah, get that shit on me, so I can fuck you up in here,'* I thought to myself. I let her ass take three steps from the table before calling her ass back.

"I'm ready to order now," I called out to her. She turned back around with a twisted look on her face. I know she was wondering why I was giving her such a hard time, but fuck her. I smirked as she snatched out her pen and pad. I looked down at the menu and waited a few extra seconds just to annoy her ass a little bit more. I placed my order and dismissed her by holding up the menu without even looking up at her. When I finally did look up, my temperature rose ten degrees. My blood pressure shot up to near stroke level. Walking in the door with a nigga on her arm was none other than my intended target, Candice. My hand instinctively dropped to my purse. I had to will myself not to take out my .38 and blow her brains out. *'Stick to the plan, stick to the plan,'* I kept reminding myself. I sat back and watched as they sat on the far end of the place. My private parts jumped at the thought of walking up to her and putting a bullet in her ass. I was so focused on mean mugging her ass that I never noticed the waitress bringing my food to the table. All the while I was eating, I fantasized about killing this hoe, but if my plan worked I wouldn't have to do that. She would kill herself. The bitch seemed to be enjoying herself, fawning all over the dude she was with. The shit was sickening to me. I called the waitress over and asked for the bill. While she was away running my credit card, I noticed a young man walk into the place with some homely looking bitch draped on his arm. He seemed to lock eyes with Candice as he walked into the place. I wanted to see what would come of it, so when the waitress brought my card back I sat there for another twenty minutes sipping a glass of water. I was shocked when the dude with Candice punched the other nigga in the stomach. When Candice and her friend left, the nigga was still on the floor yelling threats at them. From where I was sitting, he needed to close his fuckin' mouth. He had just gotten his ass whipped.

24
Candice

    I was disappointed as hell when Rashawn got a call from home telling him that he had to go back to Cleveland for a family emergency. I would've really been pissed if I hadn't gotten any dick before he left. I got up off my bed and limped toward the bathroom. I'm not going to lie, this nigga had me walking sideways. He went so deep in me that I thought his dick would crack my spine. I guess one day I will get up the nerve to let him fuck me in the ass. Although I normally welcome challenges like that, Rayshawn packed so much meat I had to think twice about having anal sex with him. After reliving my bladder, I hobbled my well fucked ass back into the bedroom and plopped back down on the bed. Ten seconds later, Toi came walking through the door with a funny look on her face.
    "The fuck you looking like that for?" I asked.
    "Bitch, I know you got my text. How come you didn't respond?"
    "Because I was getting fucked, that's why." Toi stared at me for a few seconds and then burst out laughing.
    "I shoulda fuckin' known. Bitch, you don't do nothin' but get yo' pussy pounded. You still coulda texted a bitch back and let her know you was still breathing though."
    "Why the hell would I have to do that? He's your homeboy, right? I didn't think you would hook me up with a nigga that would rape and kill a bitch."

"Nah, he wouldn't do no shit like that. He might kill that pussy though, and from the way yo' ass is sitting it looks like that's just what the fuck he's been doin'."

"Girl," I said shaking my leg from side to side, "that nigga been putting the hurt on my coochie." I got up off of my bed and limped to my mini-refrigerator.

"Damn bitch, how far did that nigga go up in you?"

"You don't even want to know," I replied, still feeling the effects of Rashawn's massive dick.

"Well, I hope you protected yo' damn self. Me and Rashawn go back but I don't keep tabs on that nigga so I don't know where that nigga's dick been."

"Huh? Oh yeah, girl hell yeah," I lied. Toi was always fussing at me about making a guy wear a rubber. And even though I knew that she was right sometimes I get so heated up that I forget all about it. I didn't feel like hearing a lecture from her so I told her what she wanted to hear.

"Oh, ok cool," she said, breathing a sigh of relief.

"But check this shit out. While me and Rashawn was getting out grub on, guess who walked the fuck up in there?" I paused for a few seconds to see if she wanted to guess. Apparently she didn't.

"Who, bitch damn?"

"Byron's punk ass came strolling up in there with some ashy ass hoe on his arm!"

"Ah hell naw! You shoulda slapped the shit outta that nigga for fuckin' up our room the way he did!"

"Please, I wasn't about to let that nigga fuck up my good time. Besides, it turned out that I didn't have to do shit. That dumb ass nigga had the nerve to come over to our table and start some shit. Rashawn tried to tell that nigga to roll the fuck out but when he got ignorant, Rashawn clocked his ass!"

"Good! That's what the fuck his bitch ass get," Toi screamed as she jumped up and gave me a high five. "You shoulda kicked him in his fuckin' face!"

"I didn't do that but I did step on his fuckin hand. You should've heard that nigga screaming like a bitch!" Toi laughed so hard at that she had to hold her stomach.

"So when did Rashawn leave?" she asked when she got done giggling.

"He left about thirty minutes ago. Girl, the way he slapped Byron's ass around, he had my pussy wet as fuck! I couldn't wait to get back here to get some of that golden rod!"

"And just what the fuck would you have done if I was here?"

"The same fuckin' thing I did do! Get me some dick, bitch!" I said laughing.

"Damn hooker!"

"Whatever! You should've been getting your pussy pounded too. Matter of fact, how come Malcom didn't come down here with Rashawn?" I asked.

"He wanted to but I told him that my parents were coming down here so he would have to make that trip another time."

My pussy jumped at the mention of her parents. I still remembered the hot threesome we'd had while she was asleep. I wonder how she would feel if she knew about that? Would she hate me or would she let me taste her pussy to see if it tasted as good as her mother's? I subconsciously shook my head, trying to get the thought out of my mind. I loved dick and I wasn't going to let that one incident turn me into a lesbian or bi-sexual. I didn't have anything against gay people, I just didn't want to be one of them.

"Damn bitch, you a'ight?" Toi asked.

"Yeah, I'm straight. Just a slight headache. So how did last night go?" I asked, changing the subject. "Since your parents were treating, I know you ate like a fucking pig."

"You better know it," she said, rubbing her stomach. "I was gonna try to get them to treat me to breakfast, but when I called their hotel room no one answered."

Just then, someone knocked at the door. At the same time, Toi's cell phone buzzed. While she answered it, I got my sore pussy ass up and made my way to the door. I didn't know about Toi, but I damn sure wasn't expecting any visitors. I opened the door and a smile popped onto my face as my aunt Charmaine walked in.

"Hey auntie," I yelled giving her a big hug. I hadn't realized until that moment how much I'd missed her. With my mother and grandmother both being dead, she was pretty much the only family I had.

"What are you doing here?"

"I came down here to see you. Plus I wanted to give you this," she said, handing me an envelope. I didn't have to look inside to know what was in it. "I figured that you may be low on cash, so here you go baby girl."

"Thanks auntie you're the best," I said, hugging her again. "You remember my friend Toi."

"Of course," she said, opening her arms wide. Toi put her mother on hold so she could hug my aunt.

"Hey Toi. How you doing?"

"I'm doing good, Ms. Charmaine. Just trying to keep my grades up."

"Now that's what I like to hear," my aunt said. "And just how are your grades coming along, young lady?"

"My grades are fine," I responded, cutting my eyes at Toi. That bitch was trying to be slick. She knew damn well my aunt was going to question me about my grades when she bought hers up.

"Mmm hmmm. We'll see when report card time comes around.

"How are your parents doing?" she asked turning her attention back to Toi.

"They doin' good. They on the line now." Toi put her phone on speaker so that my aunt and her parents could talk. Hearing the television so clearly in the background led me to believe that the phone they were using was on speaker as well.

"Hey Charmaine. How you doing girl?" Toi's mother spoke.

"I'm doing good girl. We need to get together for lunch while I'm down here."

"Sounds good to me," Toi's father cut in. "It'll have to be soon though. We're leaving in the next couple of hours."

"That's cool. My room number is 426. Give me about a half an hour, then come and get me. I'm about to leave the girls' room now."

"Hotel? You staying overnight, auntie?"

"Yeah. I need to talk to you about something," she said, looking at me with serious eyes. "Do you have a class tomorrow morning?"

"Uh…yeah, I have one."

"Well, stop by the room when you are done. We need to talk."

It seemed kind of strange to me that she would come all this way just to tell me something. I got slightly worried thinking that it was something serious, but I didn't want to jump the gun so I tried to relax. My aunt then told Toi's parents that she was on her way, gave me a hug, and headed out the door. Toi rushed her parents off the phone and ran to her side of the room and started changing clothes. It took her all of two minutes to slip into a tight white skirt.

"Damn bitch, can you breathe in that?"

"It doesn't matter," she said giving me a devilish look. "I don't plan on having it on that long," she said, winking at me.

"Nasty slut," I said teasing her.

"Whatever. You not the only one around here who can go on a dick hunt."

I laughed as Toi headed for the door. From her comment I had to assume that she was going somewhere to get her fuck on. As for me, all I wanted to do was lay back and rest me sore vagina. It didn't take me long to drift off to sleep all the while wondering what was so important that my aunt had to drive all this way to tell me in person.

25

<u>Candice</u>

I was sleeping quite peacefully until Toi's loud moans of passion woke me up.

"Oh shit baby, make me come she screamed. I glanced at my phone and saw that it was a little past six. I must've really been tired to sleep that long. I also noticed that I had five text messages form Jason. I hadn't spoken to him since he dropped me off at what he thought was the apartment I stayed in.

"Oh God, yes!" Toi yelled. I smiled, cheering my girl on as she prepared to reach her orgasm. I wondered though why I didn't hear the bed moving. Not wanting to interrupt their flow, I eased out of my bed and tip toed as quietly as I could to the edge of the wall that separated our rooms. I leaned my head around the wall and instantly had a front row seat as some dude ate Toi out. The right side of his face rested on her inner thigh. His tongue was moving so fast against her clit if it were a car it would get a speeding ticket.

"Don't stop, oooo shit muthafucka, you bet' not stop!" she commanded, gripping his bald head. Toi pumped her pelvis back and forth. The dude then slid his left middle finger inside Toi's pussy and finger fucked her as he ate her. This seemed to push Toi over the edge. She moaned so loud, I wouldn't be surprised if the whole floor heard her. Her fuck buddy's chin glistened as Toi squirted cum on his face. After spilling her love juice on his mouth, Toi tried to catch her breath, but her friend had other ideas. With Toi panting from her nut, the dude quickly slipped on a condom, climbed on top of Toi and rammed his pipe inside. I happened to get a good look at what he was working with. I have to admit, the nigga had an impressive package but he didn't have shit on Rashawn. I was hot as a firecracker. I eased back to my side of the room, climbed into my bed and spread my legs. Their nasty talk and moans had me horny as hell. My hand followed the familiar path it did when I didn't have a dick to fuck. The sensation I got from touching my swollen clit caused me to tremble. While Toi was getting dicked down on the other side of the room, I was pinching, flicking, and squeezing the hell out of my clit in an attempt to catch up to her orgasm. Sensing that my right hand needed a little help, I reached down with my left hand and started finger banging. I can't be sure but I think that me and Toi came at the same time. Her saturating a dick and me saturating my hand. The dude came a few seconds after. I would be lying if I said that I wasn't slightly jealous. I really shouldn't be though. After all, Rashawn was fucking me royally well. Heavy breathing filled the air on her side of the room. Soon after I heard someone jump out of the bed.

"Oh shit, it's after six o'clock," I heard him say.

"So?" Toi countered.

"I'm late. I have to pick my wife up from work."

"Wife? Nigga you said you had a girlfriend, not a fuckin' wife!" Toi said as if it really mattered to her.

"I did? I coulda sworn that I told you that I was married," he said, playing the dumb roll.

"Nigga you know damn well…you know what? Just get the fuck out!"

The dude didn't argue. As soon as he was dressed, he bolted out of the door. Toi walked behind him and slammed the door behind him.

"Lying muthafucka! And Candice get yo' ass up 'cause I know good and well yo' ass ain't sleep!"

'Damn. I thought I was being quiet.'

"Damn bitch, that nigga had your ass moaning loud as fuck!" I said laughing.

"And? That's what the fuck his ass was here for."

"And what the fuck you doing messing around with a married man?" I asked her.

"Look who the fuck talking. Ain't ya boy Professor Reynold's married?"

"Oh…that was different though," I said. We both laughed out loud.

"Fuck that nigga's wife," Toi said. "If the bitch was handling her business, he wouldn't been in my bed."

"True," I said, co-signing her foolishness.

"Speaking of Professor Reynold's, what's going on with that situation? Have you dumped his son yet?"

"Nah. I do have about five text messages from his ass though. I'll do it tomorrow. You know what? Let's do something tonight. Let's got to the movies or something. It's been a long time since we hung out, just me and you. Let's have a fucking girl's night out."

"Shit, I'm game. What you want to go see?"

"I don't know. Let me check my phone and see what's playing."

While Toi picked at her finger nails, I went to the internet on my cell and checked out the new movies that were showing. I don't know about Toi, but I was in the mood for something scary.

"What about The Conjuring?" I asked Toi, hoping that she was in the same mood I was in.

"Cool with me," she said.

"Let's do this shit then. The next movie is starting in an hour. That's just enough time for you to wash you fish smelling ass up."

"Bitch, fuck you," she laughed as she headed for the bathroom. While waiting for Toi to get showered and dressed, I searched for something comfortable to wear. I wasn't trying to catch a man tonight, I just wanted to chill and hang out with my girl. That didn't mean I didn't want to look fly though. I picked out a pair of hip hugging jeans to go with a tight black t-shirt. Toi was taking forever, so I grabbed my cell phone and sent Rashawn a text message telling him how great he was in the sack. Then I played around on face book while I patiently waited for Toi's slow ass. Five minutes later, Toi came back into the bedroom holding her stomach. She didn't say a word. All she did was walk over to her bed and fall backwards onto it. I hurriedly went over to her side of the room and looked down at her. Her face was twisted up and she was rubbing her stomach.

"What the fuck is wrong with you?" I asked.

"Girl I don't know. I was drying off and all of a sudden my fuckin' stomach started hurtin'?" Now I know it's selfish for feeling this way, but I was getting kind of pissed because now it started looking like we wouldn't be able to go to the damn movies.

"So now what?" I asked with an attitude. Toi must have sensed the fact that I was upset. "Look, if you really want to see the movie, I understand. Go ahead on without me."

"You sure?" I asked, not really giving a fuck if she was or not.

"Yeah, I'm sure. I can tell you really wanted to get out tonight, so take my car and go ahead. It's cool."

"Ok, girl, if you say it's ok."

I wasted no time grabbing her keys and heading out the door. I know it sounds selfish, but I didn't want to give her any chance to change her mind. As I walked out of the door, I could have sworn that I heard her call me a selfish heifer. *'What the fuck eva'*, I thought, making my way towards the elevator. I'd wanted to see this movie for a while now and since she'd given me the go ahead to watch it without her ass, I was more than happy to take her up on her offer. The fact that she'd even offered me her ride just made the situation that much sweeter. If she was expecting me to say some stupid shit like *'nah girl I don't want to see it without you'* her ass was crazy as fuck. I'd be a damn fool to let this opportunity slip away. As soon as I got outside of the safe confines of my apartment building, I became paranoid. My eyes darted to the right then the left. Byron was out there lurking around somewhere and it would be extremely stupid for me to think that he was just going to forget about what had happened at the restaurant. With Rashawn gone back to Cleveland, there was no one to stop Byron from choking the shit out of me if he saw me. I hadn't realized just how fast I was walking until I almost walked right into the car. Remembering the incident that had gone down between me, Toi, and Byron in the parking lot before, I quickly jumped in the car and locked the doors. Now I felt a little safer. After pulling out of the parking lot, I checked my watch and saw that I had almost fifteen minutes before the movie was supposed to start. During the drive there, my mind drifted to my aunt. I was tempted to call her and insist that she tell me what she wanted to talk to me about. Before my temptation could get the best of me, however, my cell phone buzzed. I frowned when I looked at the screen and saw that it was Jason. Figuring the longer I put off dumping his ass, the longer I was going to have to be bothered with him, I answered it.

"Damn baby, I been trying o get in touch with you all day," he said after I said hello.

"Yeah, I been kind of busy today," I told him, dryly.

"Oh, ok. That's cool. Listen, I was wondering if you wanted to get together tonight. A nigga hungry as fuck and I was thinking that...."

"Jason, we need to talk, boo boo," I said cutting him off. Ten seconds of silence occupied the line. I guess Jason wasn't as stupid as I thought he was. I guess he, like every other man in America, knew that when a woman told him they needed to talk, it was never good news.

"What's going on Candice?" he asked, fearfully. I opened my mouth to tell him that I didn't think we should see each other anymore but the sight of the movie theatre cut off my words. I must have been driving way over the speed limit because I got there quicker than I anticipated. Since I didn't have the time listen to him whine and beg when I informed him of our break-up, I decided to wait until after I saw the movie to kick him to the curb. He'd served his purpose.

"I really can't get into it this second, Jason. I'm doing something real important right now," I lied. "Give me an hour and a half and I will call you back." Before he could protest, I said goodbye and hung up on him. My phone buzzed twice more before I decided to turn it off completely. Fucking pest. I'd gotten my revenge on his punk ass daddy so I didn't need his ass anymore. I parked the car and got out. A light wind blew across my neck as I strutted across the parking lot. I walked into the theatre and was surprised that I was able to walk right up to the ticket window. After purchasing the ticket, I stopped by the concession stand and picked up a small bag of popcorn. I was getting excited. I loved horror movies. I settled into my seat and suffered through the many previews that were being shown. When the movie finally got started, I quickly figured out why there weren't that many people here. The movie started off dumb as hell and didn't get any better. I felt like a fool for wasting my time and money on this bull shit. The movie was so bad; I refused to stay for the ending. On my way out, I saw a couple in the back row getting their freak on. The sight immediately made me think of Rashawn's sweet meat. He hadn't been gone a full day and I was already missing the hell out of his dick. Pissed off and now horny as hell, I stormed out of the movies. I needed a drink. Hoping that Toi was feeling better I hopped in the car and headed back to the dorm. I hated drinking alone. As I eased along, I noticed that I was being followed by someone driving a white Monte Carlo. Thinking about the threats Byron hurled at me when I was leaving the restaurant, I started to get nervous. Matter of fact, I was scared shitless. I pressed the gas pedal a little harder and picked up speed hoping that I was just being paranoid. But not only did the white car do the same, it actually picked up more speed and drove up alongside of me. Bad luck then intervened as a red light forced me to stop. Even though my heart was beating a mile a minute, I tried to play it cool by not looking over towards the car. But once again, my nosiness got the best of me, forcing my head to slowly turn to the left. What I saw made my eyes pop almost completely out of my head. Although the car's window was a little more than halfway down, I was able to clearly see the barrel of a gun pointed in my direction.

"Shit!" I screamed. Instinctively, my foot pushed the gas pedal all the way to the floor. The tires squealed for a second before the power of the engine yanked the car down the street. Just a half a second after the car pulled off the back window shattered, causing glass to fly across the back seat. I almost pissed on myself as I struggled to control the fishtailing car. I was so frightened, I didn't even get a good look at who the fuck it was shooting at my ass. All I saw was that fucking barrel. Hell, truth be told that's all I needed to see! I looked in the review mirror and saw the white car trying to catch up to me. I was getting ready to panic when fate intervened and the white car was cut off by a bus. Although I didn't get a look at the driver, there was no doubt in my mind that it was Byron behind the wheel of that car. I knew he was going to be mad but shit, I didn't know the muthafucka was going to be mad enough to kill a bitch. I guess he was more pissed off and embarrassed by what happened at the restaurant than I thought. The worse part about it was that, since I didn't see who was behind the wheel, I couldn't positively identify Byron as the driver. Now I really needed a fucking drink.

26

<u>Candice</u>

I skidded to a stop, jumped out of the car, and rushed upstairs to my dorm room as fast as I could. I wasn't concerned about Byron hiding behind the building waiting to jump out and do something to me because I had left his ass in the dust a few minutes ago. I unlocked the door, went inside, and closed it behind me. I turned around and looked for Toi to let her know what had happened, but to my surprise she was nowhere to be found.

"Toi!" I yelled out before going over to her side of the room to see if she was lying in the bed.

'Where the fuck is this bitch at? I thought she said she was sick. Her ass probably out somewhere getting some dick. Lying ass hoe. Talking about she didn't feel good.'

Snatching my cell phone off of my hip, I quickly dialed Toi's number. Two seconds later, I heard her phone buzzing from her side of the room.

"What the fuck?" I yelled, frustrated. "Who the fuck leaves out without their fucking phone?" I slung my phone onto the bed and instantly regretted doing so, as it bounced of the mattress and crashed onto the floor. I took a deep breath, bent down, and picked it up. The last thing I needed to deal with was a broken phone. I thought about calling my aunt to tell her about what had happened but knowing her she would have panicked and moved down here. I didn't need a baby sitter. I jumped nervously as the door opened and Toi walked in. She had a bottle of Ginger Ale in her hand. I immediately felt like shit for thinking that she had lied to me and was out getting her pussy pounded while I was out dodging bullets. Right away she saw the look on my face and knew something was wrong.

"Yo' you alright girl?" she asked, walking up to me.

"Hell nah! Somebody fucking shot at me!"

"What? Somebody shot at you? Where the fuck was this at? You okay?"

Toi grabbed me and pulled me in close, giving me a hug that was filled with worry and love. Toi patted me down as if she was trying to see if I had any bullet holes in my body. My knees involuntarily started knocking as I thought back to my brush with death. Toi walked me over to the bed and sat me down.

"Tell me everything that happened girl."

"Shit, it's not that much to tell. All I know is that I was on my way back here from the movie when a white Monte Carlo pulled up beside me. I looked over just in time to see the barrel of the gun. I was scared shitless. I floored that bitch just before whoever it was pulled the trigger.

"Oh thank God they missed you."

"Yeah, but your back window is shattered."

"Don't worry about that shit. Windows are replaceable. Your life isn't. let's go," she said pulling me up to my feet.

"Go? Go where?"

"To the Police station. Hell, I ain't gotta be a detective to know that Byron's ass is behind this bullshit," she said, thinking along the same way I was.

"But I don't know for sure that it was him," I told her. "I never got a good look at the shooter." Toi thought for a minute. I could tell that her brain was working overtime. "You didn't see his face at all?" she asked. I shook my head from side to side. "We still should go. Even if we can't prove that it was him, they will have that shit on record."

Just as me and Toi were getting ready to walk out of the door, my cell phone vibrated. When I saw that it was Jason's pestering ass, I sent it to voice mail. His ass sure was in a hurry to get dumped. I clipped my phone on my hip and continued out the door. An hour later, me and Toi walked back into our dorm room frustrated as hell. It's not that we were surprised at what was said at the police station, but hearing it firsthand made it sound worse. Since I hadn't actually seen the shooter, they said that their hands were pretty much tied. When I brought up the notion that Byron was involved, they once again asked me if I had any tangible proof or evidence to support my claims. When I told them that I did not that was the end of that. We even saw the officer that had come to our room the first time we called them about Byron. He told us that he followed up by going to Byron's residence and asking him if he had anything to do with vandalizing our place and, just like her knew Byron would, he denied the accusation. The cops even had the nerve to tell me that technically, since I'd left the crime scene, they could cite me if they wanted to. I was furious! How the fuck are they going to cite me for getting shot at? Where they do that shit at? Only in punk ass Ohio! That was some bullshit.

"Girl you know we have to put something in the air with the day we just had," I told Toi. Without saying a word, Toi nodded and walked to her weed stash. I plopped down on the edge of my bed and rubbed my temples. My ass had barely hit the mattress before my cell phone went again. Once again, it was Jason. This time I answered it, feeling that it was time to end this charade.

"Hello," I said in an annoyed tone that caught him off guard.

"Uh…hey baby. I thought you said that you were going to call me back in an hour and a half."

"I'm still fucking busy!"

"Excuse me?" he responded, after a brief silence. Now it was time to drop the hammer on his ass.

"Jason I don't know why you can't catch the fucking hint! When I didn't call your ass back, that should have told you something! The ride was fun while it lasted boo-boo, but here is where I get the fuck off!"

"Wha…What are you saying?" his simple ass asked. He sounded so pathetic, I almost felt sorry for him.

"Nigga what the fuck does it sound like I'm saying? This shit is over, muthafucka so stop calling me!"

"But what did I do?" he whined. I could practically see the tears rolling done his cheeks.

"You're doing it now! You're being a bitch! And I don't do bitch ass niggas! Now leave me the fuck alone!" I pressed end call and hung up in his face. I honestly hadn't meant to put him down that hard but oh well. Jason was crushed, which was what I'd planned on doing all along. And the beauty of it was that even if he went to his punk ass father, crying about how I'd broken his heart, there was nothing that Professor Reynold's could do about it. If he tried to jump bad, I'd make sure that his wife got the video of us fucking. Tomorrow morning when I went to his classroom, I was going to install the final phase of my vicious plan. Blackmail.

"Girl you a fool," Toi laughed as she passed me the blunt. "You just fucked that nigga's feelings all the way up!" My cell phone went off again. And I immediately shut it off. I wasn't about to sit there and listen to his ass cry in my ear all damn night.

"Fuck that nigga and his bitch ass daddy! Professor Reynold's will think twice the next time he disrespects a bitch like me! We don't have anything to drink in here?" I asked Toi. Right on cue, she pulled a bottle of vodka from under her mattress. I looked at her and frowned.

"Hoe I know you don't call yourself hiding liquor from me. What kind of bullshit is that?"

"The kind of bullshit that makes sure that we have some now. If you woulda knew where it was, yo' alcoholic ass woulda drank it all up." I couldn't even front. She was right.

"Whatever bitch," I spat, mostly because I couldn't think of anything else to say. The two of us proceeded to sit there for the next hour and get fucked up. Damn bitch, who are you texting this time of night?" I asked when I saw her fucking with her phone.

"Don't worry about it hoe. I'm setting me up some dick for tomorrow, if it's okay with you."

"Fucking lust bucket," I teased her.

"Hey, let's hit up the bar tomorrow and score some free drinks from some suckers."

"I can't. I have to go see what my aunt wants to talk to me about."

"Oh yeah, I forgot she was still in town."

"I was actually going to call her when I got home tonight and see if I could get her to tell me what was on her mind over the phone but I got a little distracted by some asshole shooting at me."

"Are you sure whoever it was, was trying to kill you? Maybe they just wanted to scare you for some reason."

"Girl, whoever the fuck that was tried to blow my fucking brains out."

"Well, thankfully they didn't succeed." The two of us clicked glasses and took another drink.

27

Candice

The next morning my head was throbbing. I looked at the clock and was relieved to see that I had another hour and a half before I was going to drop the black mail bomb on Professor Ryenold's. I slowly sat up in my bed and reached inside my drawer for the Alka-Seltzer pack that I kept for these hangover emergencies. I was in such bad shape, the fizzing sounded like trains going through a tunnel. After downing the medication, I lay back in the bed and waited for my headache to go away. Twenty minutes later, I felt like a new woman. I jumped up, got showered, got dressed, and headed to the cafeteria. I was nervous as hell on the way there, wondering if Byron was going to try and finish the job. I grabbed a breakfast sandwich and headed straight for the Professor's classroom. But I had no intentions of going in for class. Sitting on a bench outside of the room, I ate my sandwich and turned my phone back on. It had been off since the previous night. I shook my head when I saw how many calls and text messages that I'd gotten from Jason. This nigga just didn't seem to be getting the message.

'*Baby please tell me what I did. I know I can make it right,*' one of the texts read. There were about ten more with similar messages. I deleted them all. I never even bothered to listen to the voice mail messages. We were through. Even if I wasn't doing this to get revenge on Professor Reynold's I could never be with a muthafucka that weak. I needed a strong nigga, like Rashawn. My panties instantly got wet thinking about his big dick ass. If I wasn't in a public place I may have been inclined to finger fuck myself. I was so engrossed in my thoughts about him; I hadn't noticed that the class had been dismissed. One by one the students filed out of the classroom. I waited until I was sure that the last person had left before I entered the room. Professor Reynold's had his back to the door. His cell phone was on his desk. He had it on speaker as he spoke to his wife, Felicia.

"I was calling to let you know that I found my phone," she said in an irritated voice.

"Oh yeah? Where was it at?"

"Somehow I'd left it downstairs in the basement, but I have it now."

"Felicia you know how busy I am. You couldn't tell me that when I got home?" The line went silent for a minute.

"I was just telling your ass. But since you're so fucking busy, I'll get out of your hair." Before Professor Reynolds could say another word, his wife hung up in his face.

"Dammit!" he screamed as he pounded his fist on his desk.

"I guess don't nobody like your ass now-a-days huh?" The Professor whirled around in his chair, startled. A mask of anger covered his face. With rage in his eyes, he got up out of his seat.

"I hope you're not about to do something stupid. Me and you are not the only ones who know about our little affair and if something happens to me, your wife and the police are going to have a front row seat at our little porn performance." This seemed to bring him back to his senses as he sat down slowly.

"What the hell do you want, Ms Robinson?"

"Why so formal boo-boo?" I asked, giving him a sinister smirk. "I mean, shouldn't you be calling me by one of the names you always call me? You know, bitch or whore or slut." Professor Reynodl's nostrils flared as he stared at me with beady eyes. The lust mixed with hate in them was evident.

"What do you want?" he snarled.

"Oh, I don't know. World peace. The cure for cancer. A stiff hard dick. A damn shame," I said, shaking my head. "Maybe you could've helped me out with the last one if you wasn't such an asshole." I was enjoying this so much, my pussy thumped. From the way the Professor shook, I could tell that he wanted to get up and choke the shit out of me. But the possibility of losing his loving wife as well as going to prison for doing something stupid kept his ass glued to his seat.

"Either state your reason for being here or get the fuck out!"

"Okay nigga, let's get down to business. I want two thousand dollars a month, every month until I graduate."

"What? Bitch are you out your muthafuckin' mind? I'm not paying you no two thousand dollars a month! You better go suck somebody's dick with that bullshit!" he screamed. His rants went in one ear and out the other. He was talking on pure emotion.

"I did. Your sons," I reminded him. Professor Reynold's turned two shades darker.

"You…you had sex with my son?"

"Oh nooo," I said. "I had sex with you. I fucked the shit out of your son!" I laughed. I don't know why he thought I wasn't going to screw his son. Apparently he thought that I was going to just come to his house for dinner as part of my revenge. He should have known that I was going to test drive his son's penis. "Did you know that your son's dick is bigger than yours?" I asked him as I leaned over and whispered in his ear. The Professor couldn't take it anymore. In a flash he was up and off his feet and reaching for my throat.

"Go ahead," I said to him. "Dig your own grave." Apparently the Professor wasn't listening to me at this point. He wrapped his hands around my neck and started squeezing. At that moment I began to think that I had gone too far. Spots danced in front of my eyes as he continued to apply pressure. I felt my knees weaken and my body drift to the floor. As I began to black out, I suddenly realized that I may have underestimated this man's rage.

28

<u>Byron</u>

It didn't take long for the news to get around about the fight that I'd had with Candice's friend. My teammates were on my ass about it big time. Time and time again, they had told me to leave Candice alone. That they had seen her huddled up with quite a few muthfuckas. It wasn't that I didn't believe them. I just wanted to hit the pussy. Since I didn't feel like hearing it today, I decided to just take my bitch to a hotel and peel the lining out of her pussy.

"Was it good baby?" Seka asked as she removed her mouth from my dick.

"Yeah baby, that shit was the bomb," I lied with a straight face. Truth be told, Seka's head game was terrible. The only way I could even get through it was to think about Candice's fine ass. Don't get me wrong, Seka's pussy was decent but the bitch's dick sucking skills were atrocious. She seriously needed to watch a few porno movies and tighten her game up. Time and time again, I cringed from her teeth scraping against my tool. And if that wasn't enough, she would squeeze my balls twice as hard she needed to.

"Thanks for feeding my belly baby. I was hungry as fuck," she said smiling. Seka was a nice enough girl but she wasn't what I wanted. What I wanted had embarrassed the shit out of me with that goon she was with the other day. I'd known from experience that Candice liked the pancakes there so it was no coincidence that I showed up at the restaurant that day. I was hoping to run into her but I didn't know that she was going to be with some other muthafucka. I was pissed as hell when I saw that but I did my best to keep my game face on. Since I had Seka with me, I was hoping that she would see us together and get jealous but that was far from what happened. Instinctively I ran my hand across my chin. It was sore as hell from where that muthafucka had it me. Either he was a new student on campus or someone who didn't attend the school because I had never saw him before. Seeing them together made me feel good about what I had done to Candice's room. It made me feel even better about slapping the shit out of her girl Toi. That bitch had always gotten on my nerves. She was always in our fuckin' business and never missed a chance to cock-block. That's the part I didn't understand. Both of them bitches were freaks. But Candice's pussy was something special. My original plan was to fuck them both, but once I had a sampling of Candice's sweet womb I couldn't help myself from going back and trying to get more. Seka slid her head up my stomach and let it come to rest on my chest. I grimaced when it rubbed my ribs. They were also still sore. I don't know if that nigga used to box or what but his fists felt like two sledge hammers hitting me. After a few minutes passed by, Seka reached down and started messaging my manhood.

"It's extra wet for you today daddy. You gonna give me some of this prime beef?" Without waiting for me to answer, Seka climbed on top of me an inserted my rod into her wet hot love. She was right. It was extra wet today. "Oooo yes baby, do it to me," she purred. Even though my ribs were sore I was not about to turn down some pussy. I grabbed her hips and pumped as she bounced up and down.

"You like that shit don't you girl?" I asked as I saw her eyes roll back into her head.

"Oh baby you know I like it when you stick that big dick in my hole."

Hearing her talk nasty caused my dick to get three times harder. That's the one thing that both her and Candice had in common. They loved to talk dirty during sex. Some women won't do it, but whether they know it or not that turns a man on more than any other single thing they can do.

"That's it baby! Tear this pussy up! Make yo' bitch scream! Deeper baby deeper!" Her words were music to my ears.

"You want it deeper bitch? You want me to slam that pussy?"

"Oh hell yeah baby, kill that shit!" After a couple more upward thrusts, I told Seka to get on her knees. With my dick sticking straight up in the air, I got behind her and guided my pole in. It didn't take us long to get in rhythm as I pounded her guts. Her pussy made wet swishing sounds as I tore into it. For some reason, her pussy was better today than it was the last time I fucked her. I closed my eyes and enjoyed the feeling as Seka threw her sex back on me. After a few minutes of stroking, I opened my eyes and looked straight into Candice's face. She was looking back at me licking her lips. I didn't think it was possible but my dick got even harder. Thinking about how she had played me at the restaurant, I drilled deeper.

"Is that it muthafucka? Is that the deepest you can go? You might as well get the fuck up!" She mocked. Hearing this sent me in a sexual rage. I grabbed her hips and rammed her as hard as I could.

"Is it good baby? Is this pussy good to you?"

"Oh fuck yeah Candice, you got some good ass pussy baby!" After a few more strokes, I emptied everything I had inside of her. My eyes closed and my body jerked at the sensational feeling of busting my nut. Pulling my dick out, I leaned back with both my arms on the bed, breathing heavily. When I opened my eyes back up, Seka was staring at me with the most evil look I had ever seen in my life.

"You just can't let that slut go can you?" she hissed. "What the fuck is wrong with you? Why is that bitch always on your fuckin' mind?" She asked with tears in her eyes. Time to play dumb.

"Huh? What the hell are you talking about?"

"Oh so now you gonna play stupid huh? Like you didn't just call that bitch's name while you were fuckin' me!" Since playing dumb didn't seem to work, I decided to try a different approach.

"I'm sorry baby. I just can't get over what that bitch said at the restaurant. All I was doing was going to the bathroom and that bitch had to bring up the fact that I'd accidentally killed my little brother," I lied. "The shit just came rushing back to my mind. I know it was a fucked up time for it to happen, but it did. I just feel like strangling that bitch." I rubbed my hands over my face as if I was about to shed a few tears.

"Is that right?" Seka said, folding her arms across her chest.

"I know baby," I said, putting my head down. I was beginning to think that my tactic wasn't' working until I felt Seka's hand ribbing the top of my head.

"Ok baby. I forgive you. But you gotta stop letting that bitch get in your head like that. If you want, I can call some of my cousins down here from Cincy and tighten that bitch the fuck up."

"Nah, baby I don't want you gettin' in trouble over me. I feel bad enough as it is. Tell you what. Let me go in here and use the bathroom right quick and when I come back, I'll either take you to breakfast or we can order room service. Whichever one you want to do."

I gave her a light peck on the cheek and watched her smile and blush as I walked into the bathroom trying not to laugh. When I first made up my mind that I was going to try to fuck Seka, I did a little research on her ass. I found out that she had lost her father to a violent crime so of course I used it to my advantage. By telling the false story of how my brother was brutally killed in a drive-by shooting meant for someone else, she opened her heart up to me and the rest was a piece of cake. It took all of three days to get inside her pants. Once I got inside the bathroom I couldn't contain my laughter. We were going to eat alright. But that shit was going to be on her. I had better things to spend my money on than her ass. That was too close to paying for the pussy and I definitely didn't need to do that shit. I sat down on the toilet getting ready to take a shit and evil thoughts of what I was going to do to that clown that was with Candice flew through my mind. That nigga had to get fucked up. Maybe I would just go back down to the restaurant and stake that bitch out. While I was in the bathroom I heard a knock at the room door. A few seconds later I heard Seka say hold on.

"Byron, someone's at the door asking if we need fresh towels."

"Are you serious?" I asked her. "You're really disturbing me over some bull shit like that?"

"Well damn, I was just wondering if we needed any."

"Nah Seka, we just wanna keep the same dirty ass towels," I said sarcastically.

"You ain't gotta be all sarcastic and shit. I'll get the damn towels." I gave the door the finger and shook my head. *'Bitches can be so fuckin' dumb at times,'* I thought to myself. After finishing my business, I wiped my ass, washed my hands, and made my way out of the bathroom. When I got back to the bedroom, Seka was lying on her side with her back turned to me. I guess I'd hurt her feelings and since I was ready to fuck some more, I needed to make the situation right.

"Come on girl. Don't be like that. You know I didn't mean shit by that comment." Seka didn't bulge. With the bathroom on side of the bed, it was difficult for me to see what was going on but something didn't seem right. Seka normally had some kind of slick comment whenever I said something that bothered her, but this time she remained silent. Before I could walk around the bed however, I felt someone kick me in the ass. I turned around ready to fight until I saw the pistol in his right hand pointing straight at my face. Hateful eyes stared a hole through me from behind a black ski mask.

"Nigga what the fuck you doin' in here with my wife?" he screamed.

"Wife?? Man hold the fuck up! I didn't know her ass had a fuckin' husband!" I turned my head to look at Seka. Bitch why you ain't tell me you was married? No disrespect cuz," I said after realizing that I'd just called this man's wife a bitch.

"None taken nigga. And she ain't gonna be able to answer yo' ass!"

Fear ripped through my body. My stomach turned as a creepy grin came on his mouth through the cut-out in the ski mask. Slowly I walked around the bed and almost threw up when I saw the massive amount of blood that was pouring out of Seka's neck. Her throat had been cut from ear to ear. I shook my head wondering if she could have been that stupid to open the door without looking out of the peep hole. Or maybe she did and her husband covered it. Either way, I was in deep shit. I had to find a way out of this mess or I was as good as dead.

"Listen man. I swear to God I didn't know that she was married. I didn't see a wedding ring on her finger and she sure as hell didn't say anything to me about having a husband." Keeping the gun trained on me, the masked gunman walked over to Seka, picked her left hand up, and stared at it.

"The fuck did this bitch do with the ten thousand dollar ring I bought her ass?" His head snapped up and around quickly. I hope he wasn't thinking what I thought he was thinking.

"Who in the fuck paid for this hotel room nigga?" he asked walking towards me. I hesitated and got slapped upside my head with his pistol for my trouble. "I asked yo' bitch ass a question nigga! Who the fuck paid for this hotel room?"

"I did man," I lied. I had never paid for a hotel when me and Seka went to one. She always footed the bill.

"So not only are you gonna fuck my wife and steal my money...but now you gon' lie to me too huh?"

Before I could say anything, the masked man hit me in the mouth with the butt of his gun so hard, I saw stars. The entire room stated spinning as I went down to one knee. Showing no mercy, he swiftly kicked me in the temple. My lights were ninety-five percent turned out. Suddenly I felt something sharp being dragged across my throat. Shortly after that I tried to breath but it was no use. I was choking on my own blood. The last thing I remembered seeing before I blacked out and entered hell's gates was a pair of Timberland boots leaving the hotel room.

29

Candice

Slowly and thankfully, the air started returning to my lungs. As my vision cleared, I looked up and saw Professor Reynold's back. After releasing his grip on my neck, he'd turned around and started rubbing his head. Apparently, he couldn't believe that he'd almost choked me to death. Neither could I. I blinked the tears away, desperately trying to clear my vision. Struggling to my feet, I looked at the Professor, who still had his back turned to me and eased towards the door. With my strength returning and the door in sight, I got bold again.

"You just fucked up muthafucka! Fuck a deal now! Now I'm going to expose your ass!" I broke for the door, thinking that the Professor would be hot on my heels but instead I heard his booming voice.

"Okay! You fuckin' win! Two thousand dollars a month!" I turned around and matched his angry stare with one of my own.

"Nah nigga, fuck that shit! The price has gone up since you tried to choke my ass in here! Now I want three thousand!" The Professor took a step towards me and stopped. At the same time, I took a step towards the door. If he had taken another one, I was going to bolt out of that door and go straight to a store to buy some blank discs. I wasn't playing with his ass. He shoulders drooped down, letting me know that he knew he'd been defeated.

"Is that all?" he asked in a menacing voice that would have scared me if I wasn't so mad.

"For now," I said with a smirk. "I'll be by here Friday to pick up my first payment. Nice doing business with you, bitch ass nigga," I laughed as I walked out the door.

# # #

I couldn't wait for Toi to get back so I could tell her about the sweet deal that I'd cut with Professor Reynold's. In addition to the money my aunt was sending me, I was going to be ballin' out of control when Professor Reynold's started paying me off. I nodded my head in satisfaction, feeling that he got exactly what he deserved. Aside from getting some good dick, this was the ultimate high, in my opinion. I reached over on the dresser and picked up the blunt that me and Toi had failed to finish the previous night. After firing it up, I took a long gratifying puff. I had another class to go to later, but I was thinking about just cancelling it and celebrating the rest of the day. Then I remembered that I was supposed to meet my aunt later on to find out what was so important that she had to tell me. I dialed her call number only to have it go to voice mail. Thinking that it was odd for her not to answer the phone, I called again and left her a message telling her that something came up and that we would have to postpone our meeting. Although I felt bad about cancelling on her, whatever it was could wait until the next day. I was worried at first but after thinking about it, I concluded that if it was that important she would have told me already. As soon as I sat the phone back down, it vibrated. Thinking that it was my aunt, I answered it without looking at the screen. I instantly regretted it. The voice on the other end was none other than Jason's whining ass.

"Candice, please don't hang up baby. I know whatever it is, we can work this shit out. I just know we can." This nigga was seriously started to get on my last nerve.

"Nigga didn't I tell your ass not to call me again? What the fuck part of over don't you understand?"

"But why?" He cried. "Just tell me what I did." I rubbed my temples as I listened to this wussy muthafucka whimper like a fucking bitch.

"Am I going to have to change my fucking number because you won't leave me the fuck alone?"

"No baby, please. I just want to talk. Why don't you come outside so we can talk about this."

'Outside? What the fuck this nigga doing outside of my dorm building?' I wondered. I got out of the bed, walked over to the window, and looked out. I didn't see his car anywhere. Then it hit me. I'd forgotten all about having his ass drop me off at the building down the street.

"We don't have shit to talk about!" I was starting to get very irritated.

"But I need someone to talk to right about now."

"Then call a hotline, muthafucka! But leave me the fuck alone!" I screamed into the phone just before hanging up on his ass. After doing so, I immediately turned my phone off and took another hit of the blunt. That nigga had blown the fuck out of my high with all of his crying. Begging ass muthafucka! I shook my head from side to side trying to rid my mind of his bullshit. Then I lay back in my bed and thought about Rashawn. I would give anything to have his golden rod tunneling through me right about now. My pussy moistened at the mere thought of Rashawn. I may be young but I've had quite a few sexual experiences and I've never had anyone dig my hole out like him. I slowly eased out of my pants and panties. Then I lay back on the bed and started finger fucking myself. It didn't take long for me to cum all over my sheets.

30

Charmaine

I frowned as I forced the bitter tasting coffee down my throat. "Damn, this shit is terrible," I mumbled to myself. I was sitting in the restaurant down the street from the hotel still wondering if I was making the right decision. The things I needed to tell Candice would surely have an impact on our lives, but it was a necessary evil. I looked at my watch and saw that it was time for me to take my medication. Digging into my purse, I pulled out three small bottles and popped one of the pills from each one into my mouth. Instinctively, I reached to my hip for my phone, only to remember that the battery was dead. I'd unintentionally left it unplugged before I went to bed. Because I'd been playing Candy Crush on it for an hour, leaving it unplugged had killed my battery. It was cool though. I didn't feel like arguing anymore about how I shouldn't tell Candice. I was going to tell her and that was that. The phone call I'd received last night had led to a heated conversation. But in the end, I refused to budge. My niece needed to know the truth and there was nothing that anyone on this earth could do to stop me. After finishing the eggs and hash browns in front of me I paid the bill, left a tip, and headed for the door. I got to the doorway and stopped in my tracks. Just that fast it had started raining. I made quick hurried steps to my car as the sky opened up wide and pushed the rain down on my head harder. By the time I got to my car, I was soaked. I jumped in the car as fast as I could and slammed the door shut. I was pissed.

"Fuckin' Ohio weather," I mumbled.

"Yeah, it's a bitch ain't it?" A voice sounded from behind me. My heart jumped as I turned around to see who the fuck had broken into my car. Fear overtook me when I stared into the eyes of crazy looking African American. I wanted to grab the doorknob, yank open the door, and flee for my life. I could get another car. My life wasn't for sale. But before I could execute my plan, the man raised his hand and waved a gigantic gun in my face.

"Don't even try it," he snarled.

"I don't have much money," I said, thinking that this was just a random robbery and carjacking.

"I don't remember saying that I wanted your money," he said, smiling wickedly.

"Then what do you want?" I asked, praying that he would want to rape me. I would have gladly given it up to this asshole.

"I need a ride to Cleveland later on," he said as he laughed insanely. "But first, we gonna go to my motel and chill for a while."

31

Candice

"Bitch what the fuck you doin?" I opened my eyes to see Toi standing there staring at me. She had a smile from ear to ear.

"What the fuck does it look like I'm doing?" I shot back. "Did I bother you the other day when I came in here and you were masturbating?" Even though Toi had caught me with my hand in the pussy jar, I wasn't embarrassed in the least. Shit, after what I'd pulled off today, I deserved a few good nuts. I'd already gotten off one time thinking about Rashawn's fine ass, now I was trying to get off for a second time.

"Whateva bitch. Carry on," she said, walking to her side of the room.

"Damn girl what you do, go swimming with your clothes on?" I asked, noticing her appearance. She was wet from head to toe.

"No. If you woulda looked outside instead of lying in here playing in your pussy, you woulda seen that it was raining cats and dogs."

I gave her the finger through the wall that separated our rooms. After slipping my panties back on, I got up and walked to Toi's side of the room and watched as she peeled the wet clothing off her body. I guess I shouldn't be surprised that I'm getting turned on by the flawless shape of her frame. Even though it resembled her mother's physique, the two of them didn't look anything alike in the facial area.

"Damn girlfriend, you staring awfully hard," she said.

"I was about to say something but I forgot what the fuck I was about to say," I lied.

"Yeah, ok," she said as if she knew I wasn't telling the truth. "I thought you were over there gettin' ya nut off. What's the occasion?"

"Huh?"

"Come on girl. We didn't just start living together last night. I know yo' ass. Every time something happens that makes you happy and excited you wanna bust a nut. You're words, remember?"

'Shit. I did tell her that every time I get some good news, I feel like busting a nut. I should've known that she wouldn't forget that shit.' I thought.

"Girl let me tell you," I said plopping down on her bed. It surprised the shit out me when she sat down next to me. Heat radiated off her firm wet body causing my pussy to drip. I just prayed that she didn't see it coming through my panties. I proceeded to tell her everything that had gone down with the Professor. By the time I was done, she was smiling just as much as I was.

"Now that's how you make a muthafucka pay for his bullshit," she said, giving me a high five. "Now you can get my damn back window fixed," she said laughing. "Let me run take a shower right quick and we can pour us a couple of drinks to celebrate."

Pre-cum continued to ooze out of my cunt as Toi disappeared through the door and headed for the bathroom. I fell back onto her bed and tried to get a grip on my emotions. Elation at the victory over the Professor was replaced by sexual energy as flashbacks of the sinful threesome I'd participated in entered my mind. My panties got wet as I fantasized about sitting on Toi's face or vice-versa. I could just feel her hot wet tongue penetrating my sex lips and slapping my clit from side to side.

'This can't be happening to me,' I thought. *'I'm not gay.'*

I tried to convince myself that these feelings I was having for Toi were not real. That they were just a figment of my imagination. But apparently my body didn't get the memo. Heat surged through me as I removed my panties and slung them on the floor. A soft moan escaped my lips as I reached between my legs and inserted my middle finger into my vagina. Licking my lips, I pumped in and out. Then I let my finger travel upward and come to a stop at my love bump. My body trembled as I started flicking my clit. "Ooooo, shiiittt," I moaned, feeling my release building up. I slowed down, not wanting to come yet, but wanting to enjoy the fantastic sensation I was giving myself. I was in heaven as I reached up with my right hand and cupped my left tit. I leaned my head forward at the same time I pushed my breast upward and stuck my tongue out. Since my clit was receiving so much attention from my left hand, I saw no reason for my nipples to be neglected. I bit my bottom lip and pinched the areola. A sudden thought occurred to me. If Cathy's pussy tasted that good, I wondered if mine tasted just as good. Here I had been wondering about how Toi's goodies tasted and I hadn't even sampled my own. With a smile on my face, I reached up and stuck my finger in my mouth. I sucked on it sensually, trying to devour every drop of juice on my finger. I jumped and my eyes popped open as I felt something sliding into my pussy. Lying next to me with a lustful grin on her face was Toi. Since her fingers were longer than mine, she went a little deeper than I could go myself. Before I could even comment on her being there, Toi upped the ante by sticking two fingers inside me.

"Shit!" I cried out as she pleasured me. "Toi, what the hell are you doing?"

"Bitch please," she said softly as she nibbled on my ear. "You know damn well this is what yo' ass been wantin'."

I couldn't deny it. She was right. Her finger fucking me was part of my fantasy with her. But now that it was actually taking place, I was slightly embarrassed that she knew my feelings. The bed we were in was small, so we had no choice but to be close to each other. I was just about to come when Toi somehow flipped my body over so that I was on top of her. With light force, she grabbed the top of my head and pushed it down. I didn't resist. I opened my mouth and covered one of her dark brown nipples, sucking on it smoothly and gently biting it at the same time.

"Oh go ahead girl, eat my pussy," she purred. Even though I was afraid that what we were doing might eventually ruin our friendship, I just couldn't stop myself from dropping my head below her waist. Toi's back arched as I began to munch on her carpet. "Oh fuck yes, stick your tongue in there," she moaned. She didn't have to ask twice as I jabbed my licker into her wet cum cave. Her hairy pussy was damn near smothering me as she pushed my head further into her sex. I was enjoying every minute of it. Just like I thought her pussy tasted just as good as her mothers.

"Oh shit, that's it! That's it baby! Make mama cum!" Toi urged me on as I proceeded to lick faster and faster. Toi grabbed a handful of my hair as she drenched my mouth and chin with her hot love.

"Damn Candice, that shit was the bomb," she said as she rolled off of the bed and started getting dressed.

"Uh excuse me but aren't you forgetting something?" I asked with an attitude.

"What the fuck you talkin' about?" she responded, still panting from the tongue whipping I'd just put on her clit.

"Oh so you're not going to return the favor huh?"

"I'll do it later on. I'm already late for a class."

"What? Where they do that shit at? What kind of dirty shit is that?"

"Girl, don't even act like that. I told you that I'll hook you up later on."

"You damn right you will!"

I was heated. Just five minutes ago, this bitch had just gushed cum all over my face and down my throat. And now she wanted to act like she was in a fucking rush. I opened my mouth to give her a piece of my mind but was interrupted by a knock on the door. Still shaking my head at the shady shit Toi had just pulled on me, I got up, ran to my side of the room, and threw some clothes on.

"Okay, you don't have to be a bitch about it," she said as I bumped her shoulder on the way. I ignored her and opened the door. Standing there in the doorway were the same cops that were there before. I looked at Toi and then back at them.

"Yes, may we help you?" I politely asked.

"Can we come inside please?" The dyke looking cop asked, taking the lead. Her demeanor was somewhat different than it was the last time they were here. The two of them stepped inside with serious looks on their faces.

"We need to talk to you about Byron Crawford."

"Well it's about damn time," I shouted. "Y'all need me to make a statement so you can arrest his ass? Hell, he did trash our place and shot at me yesterday."

"Were you present at this shooting?" he asked her.

"Well, no I wasn't,' she answered hesitantly. I couldn't blame her though. These two cops looked like they were all business.

"Are you sure it was Byron Crawford that shot at you, Ms. Robinson."

"It had to be him," I said, a frown forming on my face.

"And why is that?"

"Because he's the only one I had beef with!"

"Oh, I see. Tell me something, Ms. Robinson. Did you actually see who it was that shot at you?" I twisted my lips up. He already knew the answer to the question, so I don't know why the fuck he was even asking it.

"No, I didn't," I hissed, folding my arms.

"Then you can't be sure that it was even Mr. Crawford that shot at you, can you?"

"No, I guess I can't."

"Officer, what is this all about?" Toi asked.

"Ms. Robinson, when is the last time you saw Mr. Crawford?" the dyke bitch asked, ignoring Toi completely.

"At a restaurant."

"Which restaurant?"

"Pancake Heaven."

"Did you two interact with each other?"

"I don't remember."

"Really? So nothing happened that we should know about?" I looked at Toi nervously. "Ms. Robinson, if something happened, it's best that you tell us now. If we find out later on that you were not forthcoming with us, it could get you into a lot trouble later on."

"Look, him and a friend of mine got into an altercation, but it wasn't a big deal okay?"

"What is this friend of yours name?"

"Rashawn." the officer scribbled in his pad, stopped, and stared at me for a few seconds. "This friend of your gat a last name?"

"I don't know his last name." The dyke cop raised an eyebrow. It was obvious that she thought I was lying to them.

"Really? You don't know his last name?" She asked.

"No, I really don't," I said trying to convince them. Now I was starting to get scared. There was something going on here that they hadn't shared with us yet. "I met him a couple of weeks ago while I was in Cleveland. Then he came down here to visit me and we had had breakfast."

"Breakfast huh?" The dyke smirked.

"Yeah, breakfast," I said smartly. "And that's when the altercation occurred. Now will you guys please tell us what's going on?"

"Ms. Robinson, the reason we are asking these questions is because there has been a terrible tragedy. I don't know if you are aware of it or not but Byron Crawford, along with someone we believe to be a companion of his, was found dead in a hotel a few hours ago. Is it your contention that you had nothing to do with this?"

I exploded.

"Why in the hell would you ask me some bullshit like that?"

"I think you already know the answer to that Ms. Robinson. Are you sure that you had nothing to do with Mr. Crawford's death?"

"What part of hell no don't you understand, the hell or the no?"

I knew I wasn't doing myself any favors by talking to the police in a disrespectful manner, but I was shocked and outraged. Byron was an asshole and I had grown to dislike him to the pint of hating his ass, but I had nothing to do with him getting killed. That ass whipping that Rashawn had put on him was more than satisfying for me. And here these two clowns were standing in front of me accusing me of murder. The male cop continued to stare at me as he put his note pad away. The two of them then headed for the door.

"Don't leave town. We may have a few more questions we need to ask you," the dyke said as they left. Me and Toi stared at each other for a few seconds. No one said a word as each of us stood there wondering what had happened to Byron.

"I need a fuckin' drink," Toi finally said, breaking our silence.

"Pour me one too," I said. I was nervous as fuck. I couldn't believe that they actually thought I had something to do with Byron's ass getting killed. A few seconds later, Toi walked up to me and handed me a glass filled to the rim. From the color of the drink, I could tell she had cut the vodka with cranberry juice. Upon further inspection of the color, I noticed that it was a lighter shade of red than normal. But after taking a sip, I saw why it was.

"Damn," I cried out. "This shit strong as fuck!"

"Shit, after what we just went through, I felt our drinks needed a little extra kick. That's it for the liquor though. I'm gonna have to run to the store and get some more,"

"You're not going to class?" I asked her.

"After that shit? Hell nah! I'm gonna get us something to toss back and chill here with you for the rest of the night. You my girl, I ain't gonna leave you hanging like that."

That made me feel a whole lot better. While Toi was gone, I decided to call my aunt and see if she'd gotten my message about not being able to meet with her today. I hadn't heard back from her so I hoped that she wasn't mad at me. Just as I was about to call her, she texted me.

'Emergency back in Cleveland. Someone tried to break into the house. Alarm went off and scared him away but the front door is broken. Neighbors are watching the house for me until I get back. Will call you later.'

"This fucking day just keeps getting better and better," I mumbled to myself. I shook my head as I sipped on the potent liquor. I sat back and thought about how things had gone from sugar to shit for me in less than three hours. My eye lids became heavy as I sipped more of the vodka. By the time I was almost done with it my drink, my body was ultra-relaxed. I sat my glass down on the night stand and lay back. The events of the day had completely worn me out. The entire world came to a grinding halt for me as the sandman wrapped his arms around me and dragged me into his world.

Next Door Nympho 2

32

__Candice__

My eyes popped open. I looked around trying to gain my bearings. For one brief minute, I had no idea where I was or what I was doing there. But ever so slowly, the fog started to lift from my mind. My brain began to engage my thoughts. The last thing I remembered was sitting on my bed sipping that gasoline that Toi called a drink. If she was trying to put me out for the count, that cranberry/vodka mix more than did the trick. My head pounded as I tried to sit up in the bed. Not wanting it to get any worse than it already was, I gave up the fight and lay back down. I was definitely going to have to take an Alka-Seltzer or two this morning to ward off the hangover demon. I glanced at the clock and saw that it was nine-thirty. Knowing that Toi had a class in ten minutes, I opened my mouth to yell to her side of the room but quickly changed my mind.

'The fuck am I doin,' I thought to myself. *'I have a massive hangover and I'm about to yell across the fucking room. If her ass isn't up, then too fucking bad.'*

I opened my night stand drawer, grabbed a pack of medicine, opened it, and popped it into my mouth. Then I picked up the bottle of water on the night stand and took an extra large gulp hoping that it would dissolve the Alka-Seltzer on the way down. I knew this wasn't the correct way to take Alka-Seltzer but my head was pounding. I didn't have time to put that shit in water and wait for it to dissolve. Forty five minutes, I opened my eyes again. I must have fallen asleep because it damn sure didn't seem like I'd laid back down for that long. Feeling sluggish I got up and dragged myself to the bathroom. The realization that Toi wasn't in the room had pretty much convinced me that I had indeed fallen back asleep. I'm a little surprised that Toi didn't try to wake me up when she came back with the liquor the previous night. But then again maybe she had and I didn't or couldn't respond. I must have been more exhausted than I thought. I needed to get up and get my day started so I climbed in the shower and let the hot water massage my body. The water seemed to refresh me. I got out feeling like a new woman. I was still slightly shaken over what had happen to Byron, but there was nothing I could do about it. Even though the cops had made me nervous with all of their accusing questions, deep in my heart I knew that I didn't have anything to worry about. I didn't have anything to do with Byron being murdered. I couldn't help but wonder who did it though. I looked at the clock and it gave me a wicked idea. Today was the day that Professor Reynolds was conducting tutoring sessions in his classroom. Just for shits and giggles, I decided to swing by there and annoy him. Since there was going to be other students there, I was fairly convinced that he would keep his hands to himself. After getting dressed I darted out the door and headed straight for the Professor's classroom. When I got there however, disappointment washed over me. His door was closed and there was a note attached to it.

'Tutoring sessions have been cancelled until further notice.'

"Ain't that a bitch?" I mumbled under my breath.

"I hear you girl," a short light skinned girl standing behind me said. "I think he's gonna be out awhile too."

"Oh yeah? Why is that?" I asked.

"Oh you haven't heard? Professor Reynolds had a mild heart attack this morning. They don't know when he'll be back."

'A heart attack?' I thought. *'There didn't seem to be anything wrong with his heart when we were fucking'.*

"Is he going to be okay?"

"I think so, but you know the doctors are going to take extra precaution with him."

'Ah man. That nigga can't be dying,' I thought. *'I need that bread from his ass,'*

The girl wanted to talk some more but I was done listening to her ass. I turned and walked out of the building feeling bummed out that I was apparently about to miss out some money. I know it sounds cold, but oh well. I'm a selfish bitch. Not having anything to do for a few hours, I decided to fuck around on social media. I reached for my phone only to discover that it wasn't on my hip. Then I remembered that I'd left it in my dorm room. It was no big deal though, since I was on my way back there anyway. Once I got back to my room, I stretched out on the bed and powered my phone back up. Waiting for me was a picture text message from my aunt. I smiled, thinking that it was probably a photo of her posing like she was known to do. But once I opened it up, the smile on my face turned to pure horror. Sitting side by side tied up in chairs were my aunt Charmaine and my best friend Toi. Both of them were blindfolded and gagged. Toi had a cut on her cheek that indicated that she had been hit. Five seconds later, another text came through. This time it was a message.

'Bring your little slutty ass to your aunt's house in Cleveland. We have unfinished business. And remember...you are being watched. If you call the cops, this old bitch and the young tramp are as good as dead!

You will find Toi's car keys in the glove compartment of her car. Now get your as here...NOW!'

"Oh my God," I said as I started shaking. My first thought was to call the police, but I had to take the threat about killing my aunt and best friend seriously. Even though I didn't want to worry them, I felt that it was only right to call Toi's parents and let them know what was going on. Maybe they could come up with a solution to get our loved ones out of this mess. I called twice and it went to voice mail both times. The third time I called, I tried to leave a message but the mail box was full. I was on my own.

33

Candice

    The cold wind whipped across my neck as I rolled across the highway. I tried as hard as I could to contain the tears that were watering up my eyes and trying to blind me. The last thing I wanted to do was to crash before I got a chance to help my aunt and best friend. I couldn't believe the fucked up way my life had spiraled out of control in the last hour. I'd gone from possibly making three thousand dollars a month to praying that my aunt and BFF were not killed by some unknown maniac. From the time I'd hit the highway I'd been racking my brain trying to figure out who could be behind something this sinister. A sudden thought occurred to me. Maybe Rashawn could help. I know it would be asking a lot of him to get so deeply involved in my troubles but I was desperate. I didn't have anywhere else to turn and no one else to turn to. Plus, Toi was his friend too, so he would probably be glad to help. I dialed his number and waited patiently for him to pick up.

    "Hello," he answered sleepily.

    "Rashawn! Thank God you answered baby!"

    "Candice?"

    "Yes, it's me! Listen, I need you to do me a favor. I need you to meet me at my aunt's house on Parkgate!"

    "What's wrong baby? Are you in some kind of trouble? You need me?" Immediately I relaxed a little bit. It felt so good to have him in my corner.

    "Yes baby, I need you."

    "Ok. Give me the address."

I rattled off the numbers for him and told him that I would meet him there in ten minutes. He said that he was in that area so it wouldn't take him that long. After hanging up from him I got off the freeway and headed towards my aunt's house. I was nervous as fuck. I briefly wondered if I was making a mistake by not calling the police but I would never be able to forgive myself if I did and the threat against my aunt and friend was carried out. A sudden flashback passed through my mind. Of all the times to be thinking about giving Rashawn some head, the vision of me sucking his dick on the way back to my dorm room the other day ran through my mind. I quickly shook it off. I couldn't afford to be distracted by my lewd thoughts right now. The lives of the people I cared about were hanging in the balance. After hanging up from Rashawn, I pulled off the freeway and headed straight for St. Clair Avenue. That was the fasted route to get to my aunt's house. Once I got there, I had to force myself to slow down. I didn't want to risk getting pulled over by the police but I probably wouldn't have stopped anyway. I had to get to aunt Charmaine's house no matter what. The stoplights seemed to take forever. Sweat formed on my upper lip as I made my way through the city streets. It had been a long time since I'd driven these pot hole filled roads. I can't say that I missed it one bit. I started perspiring a little more as I made a left on 105th and headed towards my destination. My chest started to tighten. I made a right on my aunt's street and forced myself to slow down. I felt slightly better when I saw that Rashawn was already there.

  Maybe he had surprised the asshole that'd sent me that picture and message and was waiting for me. Just before I got out of the car, I glanced down and saw my switchblade lying on the passenger's side floor. I thought I had left it at Toi's parent's house, but apparently I'd left it in Toi's car. I hadn't noticed it before. It was probably under the seat and slid out when I jammed on the breaks and came to a sudden stop. I put it in my back pocket, jumped out of the car and ran up on the porch as fast as my twenty year old legs would carry me. I reached for the door knob but it was locked, forcing me to have to dig my key out of my pocket. For some strange reason, the flashback of me giving Rashawn a blowjob after we left the Pancake House popped into my head again.

With more important things to worry about, I pushed the thought completely out of my mind. I opened the door and ran into the house expecting the worse but praying for the best. I was momentarily confused as I looked around and didn't see anyone. I proceeded to walk upstairs and stood in the hallway. Suddenly my aunt's bedroom door swung open. Rashawn stepped out and motioned for me to come towards him. I breathed a sigh of relief as he nodded that everything was okay. As soon as I followed him into the room, my confusion returned stronger than before. My aunt was sprawled out on the bed; face down in her birthday suit. She was still blindfolded and gagged. Toi was seated in a chair facing the door. Her feet were bound and her hands were behind her back.

"Rashawn, what the hell is going on?" I asked as I turned around to face him. Rashawn didn't answer. He just stared at me with empty eyes. Then, all of a sudden, a few things hit me. Why did I need to use my key? In her text message my aunt said that the door had been broken. She hadn't had time to get it fixed, especially with what was happening now. Also, after me and Rashawn had left Pancake Heaven, he had called Byron by name. I'd never told him Byron's name. I only said he was a dude I used to date. This was a set-up. Rashawn had some unknown vendetta against me, my aunt, and Toi. He had orchestrated this whole thing and I had no idea why. He had used his friendship with Toi to get close to me.

"Why, Rashawn?"

"Sorry baby," he said just before my lights were turned out.

34

Candice

My head felt like it was going to split in two. The constant throbbing between my ears made me wish I was still unconscious. My legs were tied to both legs of the chair I was seated in. My hands were tied behind my back but didn't loop around the chair. Thinking that the pain would increase, I was afraid to open my eyes. I was even more afraid of what I might see. But I had to know. Slowly and fearfully I opened my eyes. My aunt was still spread eagled face down on her bed. She was still blindfolded, gagged, and butt assed naked. I looked to my right and saw that I was seated next to my aunt's dresser drawer, about five feet from the side of the bed. Whatever Rayshawn had planned on doing to my aunt, he wanted me to have a front row seat. Just as I began to wonder what he'd done to my friend, the door opened and in she walked. She had a pistol in her hand as Rashawn followed behind her looking like her body guard.

"Toi, what the fuck is going on here?" With blinding speed, Toi ran across the room and back handed the shit out of me.

"Shut the fuck up! This is all your fault for having a slut for a mother!" she yelled. I had no idea what she was talking about. How did she know my mother? "Now, since I can't inflict pain on your tramp of a mother, I guess you will have to do! Rashawn, do what you do best!"

Rashawn looked at me smiled. He then took off his pants and started stroking his dick. It became hard instantly. I felt ashamed that I was getting wet during a situation like this.

"Nigga quit playing and do what the fuck I'm paying you to do," she yelled at him. Then it hit me. Rashawn wasn't the ring leader in this shit. Toi was, and I didn't know why. Rashawn cut his eyes at her, letting her know that he didn't appreciate being talked to like that. "Nigga do you want to get paid or not?" She asked him.

Rashawn didn't answer. Instead he crawled up behind my helpless aunt and slammed his dick inside of her. The gag on her mouth couldn't contain the screams that he'd forced out of her by pounding her womb. All during the rape, Toi stood there with a wide grin on her face. Rashawn then pulled his dick out of her and looked at me with a sinister snarl.

"Since you wouldn't let me fuck you in the ass, I guess I gotta take it out on your aunt." Before I could beg him not to, Rashawn sodomized my aunt. My aunt screamed in pain. I closed my eyes. My heart couldn't take seeing the agony etched in my aunt's face.

"Bitch, open yo' eyes before I blow yo' fuckin' brains out!"

I did as I was told. My heart tore as I was forced to watch Rashawn rip open my aunt's anal cavity. Blood covered his dick as he pounded away. "Rashawn, please stop!" I begged him. He ignored me and continued his assault. Then I thought about the knife in my back pocket. If I could get to it and cut my hands free, we might have a chance, especially since I knew that my aunt kept a gun in the drawer I was sitting next to. I looked at Toi who was enjoying this sick show. Trying not to use a lot of motion, I eased my hand into my back pocket. I carefully slid the knife out, clicked it open, and maneuvered it so that the blade was touching the rope that held me. Back and forth I moved the blade until I heard small pop indicating that I'd cut through. I looked at Rashawn and knew that he was close to coming. I had to hurry. I looked over at Toi and saw that her perverted ass was squeezing her breast. I thought I was bad. Seeing that she wasn't paying me much attention, I eased the drawer open and grabbed the gun. Since she'd started coping feels on herself, she'd laid her gun down. As I eased the gun out of the drawer, I noticed an envelope addressed to me. I would make sure to ask my aunt about it if we made it out of this alive. Rashawn moaned loudly as his body jerked. He was coming. I made sure it was his last but as I pointed my aunt's .380 caliber semi-automatic and fired three shots into his chest area. Then, before she could grab her gun off the dresser, I fired at Toi. The bullet struck her in the middle of her chest. Toi staggered back against the closed bedroom door and slid down to the floor. The gun fell out of her hand. Seeing that I was no longer in danger, I grabbed the knife I'd sat down in the chair next to me and cut my legs free. I jumped up and hurried over to my aunt.

"Auntie! Are you okay?" I asked, ripping the gag from her mouth and pulling he blindfold from her eyes. Tears flowed down her cheeks.

"No baby, I'm not. You need to call an ambulance." I did what my aunt told me and then stomped over to Toi. This bitch had some explaining to do.

"Why Toi? Why in the fuck would you do this shit to me? I thought youn were my friend!" With blood pouring from her chest, Toi lifted her cold eyes towards me.

"Fuck you," she said. "You're piece of shit mother caused me great pain. Now I'm gonna return the favor. I may die on this floor, but your death is gonna be twice as bad. You see that muthafucka over there with the holes in his chest? The nigga you been fuckin' on a regular basis? Well, that fool is HIV positive." My heart nearly stopped. Was she bluffing? It had to be a bluff.

"I don't believe you," I said.

"I don't give a shit if you do or don't. And as far as everything else goes, ask that bitch over there," she spat. "I ain't tellin' you shit."

Toi then coughed up blood and passed out. Looking for answers, I reached into Toi's pockets and pulled out a piece to the puzzle.

# # #

My heart raced a mile a minute as I sat in the emergency room's waiting area. Every time a doctor came out of the back, it skipped a beat. Rashawn had pretty much ripped my aunt's insides to shreds. She had been in surgery a little over two hours. While the doctors were busy trying to repair the damage, I had time to think and reflect on what had happened. After digging around in Toi's pocket, I pulled out two pictures. One was of my mother. It had been slightly torn and scratched up. The other photo almost caused me to vomit. It was a picture of Hank. Hank was the man who'd accused my mother of infecting him with HIV. Several years ago, he'd broken into me and my grandmother's house, threatened us at gunpoint, and raped my aunt. All in the name of revenge. Hank was determined to get even with my mother. Lucky for us, our next door neighbor was a nosey old bird who had heard the commotion and decided to call the cops. Hank had just got done raping my aunt when we heard the sirens. He bolted out the back door but was caught by an officer who'd come around the back. Hank was arrested and charged with rape, breaking and entering, and menacing. He never made it to trial though. While awaiting his court date, Hank was stabbed to death in the county jail. But even as I stared at the picture and traveled down memory lane, I was still confused. I still had no idea what Hank, my aunt, my mother, and Toi all had in common with each other. But after tearing open the envelope that my aunt had addressed to me and reading the letter inside, it all became crystal clear. Pure shock was the only way to describe the feeling I felt while reading it. The nuts and bolts of the story is that my aunt Charmaine was Toi's birth mother. She gave Toi up for adoption when Toi was a baby. At the time, aunt Charmaine had no desire to know who was adopting Toi. She herself was young and wild, much like my mother. But she made sure to tell the adoption agency that she wanted to keep tabs on Toi. And from what the letter says, my grandmother never even knew aunt Charmaine had gotten pregnant. Apparently my aunt stayed into it with my grandmother on purpose so she could use that as an excuse to stay away. When Toi became a teenager, she was approached by my aunt in a mall. My aunt proceeded to tell Toi who she was and why she gave her up. When Toi asked about her father, aunt Charmaine lied and told her that he was dead. Over time guilt ate at her and she finally told her that her father was alive. Although Toi was pissed at her for abandoning her and lying about her father being dead, she was willing to forgive aunt Charmaine if she would set up a meeting so she could finally meet him. My aunt slickly set it up, telling Hank that she wanted to see him again. Hank had no idea that she was going to bring Toi, nor did he know that he'd even fathered a child. By this time Hank was secretly messing around with my mother. Just three days before aunt Charmaine was going to introduce Toi to her father, the break-in and rape incident occurred. Hank had no idea that my mother and aunt Charmaine were sisters at first. He'd met my mother at a bar one night and the two of them started up a sexual relationship. Now that I think about it, I remember him saying something about it being just like old times when he was raping my aunt, but until now I'd never thought about it. When Hank got killed, Toi snapped. After hearing about what had happened at my grandmother's house, she blamed my mother and my aunt for what had happened and held them responsible for not ever getting the chance to meet her father. She tricked her mother into thinking that she wanted to meet me because we were cousins and she wanted to get to know me. All the while she was plotting her revenge. When she heard that I attended Kent State, she immediately applied. Since my mother was dead, Toi decided to take it out on me by setting me up with a man who was HIV positive. It stood to reason that that was why she was holding the condom wrapper and telling at Rashawn when we were at Malcom's house. She was pissed because we had used a rubber, which protected me from infection. I still couldn't understand how she ended up as my roommate though. Maybe she fucked the person in charge. The sad truth about this mess surfaced in the last paragraph of the letter. My mother didn't give Hank HIV. Aunt Charmaine did, although she didn't do it intentionally. In the letter she never states where or who she got it from. She ended the letter by telling me that she was sorry for taking so long to tell me and that she hoped that someday I could find it in my heart to forgive her. After reading the letter, I folded it up and put it back in my pocket. I really didn't know what to feel. Part of me was angry and part of me was relieved to know the truth. "Family for Charmaine Robinson," I heard the doctor say. I got up and walked up to the short African American woman. She put her hand on my shoulder and tried to comfort me while telling me that my dear sweet aunt was dead.

Next Door Nympho 2

Epilogue

Candice sat on the couch in the middle of the living room eating a pretzel. It had been a little over a month since she had buried her aunt and it just wasn't in her heart to keep going to school. She did plan on going back at some point but for now she just didn't have the energy or the will. Candice looked at her watch and frowned. The pizza delivery guy was fifteen minutes late and her stomach was starting to growl. Her cell phone chirped, further annoying her. He was watching her favorite movie and didn't want to be disturbed. She looked at the screen and set the phone back down on the sofa. Even though she was appreciative of Javis and Cathy checking up on her, she just wasn't in the mood to talk. Candice had slightly twisted the version of events when she explained to them what had happened. Even though Toi turned out to be a manipulative bitch, Candice felt there was no reason for them to know that so she embellished the truth. Candice's stomach growled again. She was going to give them five more minutes the. She was going to call the pizza place and go off. She'd ordered pizza every Friday night since moving back into her aunt's house, so she couldn't understand what was taking them so long. Just as she picked up her phone to call and read them the riot act, the doorbell rang. "About fuckin time," she complained. Candice grabbed the ten dollars she had lying on the table. She liked ordering from this particular company. Not only did the pizza taste good, it was cheap. She usually tipped the delivery man a few bucks but since she had to wait on him, she wasn't going to do it this time. She opened the door ready to complain to him about his tardiness but didn't get the chance. Candice crumbled to the floor after being smashed in the face with a hammer. Every bone in her nose was crushed. Blood poured from her face like a broken faucet. With Candice screaming in pain, a figure stood over her holding the bloody tool.

"Did you really think you would destroy my family and I wouldn't find you?" Felicia asked. Her voice dripped with malice. Since Candice hadn't been back to school, she had no way of knowing that Professor Reynolds had died from the heart attack he'd had. She was so distraught about her aunt, she'd completely forgotten about the blackmail money. Rage flashed in Felicia's eyes as she remembered the picture messaged she received from Candice. Felicia and her husband's phone numbers were only one number apart so when Candice sent the message it went to Felicia's phone instead of the Professor. When Felicia saw it, she lost it. Neither Candice nor Toi ever considered the fact that it was Felicia who had fired the shot at Candice. Toi, who thought her chance at getting revenge on Candice was slipping away, mistakenly thought that Byron was the one who had shot at Candice and had Rashawn kill him to get him out of the way. Felicia hit Candice in the head twice more before pulling a newspaper from her back pocket. Candice died without ever reading the headline.

'Prominent Professor dies the same day his son commits suicide. Wife says sin complained of a broken heart.'

The End

1. Who do you think was worse, Candice or her mother Diamond in part one?
2. Did you know that the unknown person was Toi?
3. Were you able to figure out who shot at Candice?
4. Do you think Candice took it too far in regards to paying back Professor Reynolds?
5. Should Charmaine have told Candice mush sooner?
6. Do you think Candice should have been able to see through Rashawn?
7. Were you able to figure out that it was Rashawn who killed Byron and Seka?
8. Did it surprise you that Charmaine died?
9. Who's the bigger slut, Candice or her mother?
10. Did you catch it when Rashawn called Byron by name outside of the restaurant even though Candice hadn't said Byron's name yet?
11. Did you suspect Felicia of shooting at Candice?
12. What did you think about Jason committing suicide?
13. Did you feel sorry for Jason or is all fair in love and war?